Unending Rooms

UNENDING
ROOMS

stories

Daniel Chacón

Black Lawrence Press
New York

Black Lawrence Press
www.blacklawrencepress.com

Black Lawrence Press
8405 Bay Parkway C8
Brooklyn, N.Y. 11214
U.S.A.

Published 2008 by Black Lawrence Press, a division of Dzanc Books
Book design by Steven Seighman

First edition 2008
ISBN: 978-0-9815899-3-0

Printed in the United States

This is a work of fiction. Any resemblance to actual persons, living or dead, or events is entirely coincidental.

for Sasha

My sister, my bride!

ONE

it. Her lips are very red, very plump. She was dressed nice, too, but you could tell she was poor by the way the hems of her clothes were unraveling."

"Probably on welfare too," says Vern.

"You have a lot of room to criticize," says Shelly. "Mr. Freeloader. Mr. Still-Lives-With-Mommy."

"Hey, Screw you," says Vern. "I contribute around here. I pay rent."

"What, fifty dollars a month?"

"Let him finish," says Kevin from the kitchen.

"So, it's obvious that Santa Claus, the bus driver, doesn't want to stop for me and Paco," I say, "because of the way we're dressed. And maybe he saw our tattoos."

Mine's on the forearm, letters and numbers, and one on my neck, an image of a growling bulldog.

"And this was the time when they had that policy," I continue, "that if you looked like a gang member, the bus drivers didn't have to stop for you. I'm not sure if it was legal, but that's the way it was.

"But there's this young Mexican mother with her child, so Santa Claus stops. Paco lets her go first, the baby in her arms, so he can watch her climb the stairs. She forgets the stroller on the sidewalk. The bus driver asks her what she's going to do, but he's looking at Paco when he says it. The mother squeezes by Paco and gets the stroller, squeezes by Paco again and carries it on."

"How come you didn't help her?" asks Kevin.

I look at my little brother. He's half Japanese, half brother to us all. Vern, Shelly and I are Chicanos. Kevin's black eyes are as wide as walnuts. He wants to go to the same university where I attend. And major in History, too. I try to explain it to him.

"Paco and I were always. . ."

"Oh my, correct grammar," says Vern. "Paco and *I*."

"People try really hard not to look at us, but everyone does. If they're little kids or old ladies, well that's O.K., let them look, because mostly they're wondering what you might do. It's attitude. I couldn't help this lady."

"That's a shit-poor excuse," says Vern.

"You're right," I say, "it is. What happened next, I mean, that's what it was. This was three years ago. Not long after this day I said to myself, the heck with this. I went to junior college and now, well, you know where I am now."

"You make it sound like you're all successful," says Vern. "You ain't shit."

"Stop it, Vern," says Shelly. "He's accomplished a lot. You never even finished junior college or held a job for more than a month."

"UC Santa Cruz is a great school," says Kevin. "You should be proud of your brother."

"Proud of Affirmative Action Boy? I don't think so."

"So what happened next?" says Shelly.

"Paco hands the money to Santa Claus, who says, 'Where are you going?' Paco says he's going to visit his mama. Santa looks at him like he hates him, but he takes the money anyway. We're walking to the back of the bus. And it's full of people, mostly old ladies doing their shopping, so there are hardly any seats left, some in the back, three of them. So Paco runs to the back to get them before the girl does, running right by her because that's where she was heading. She stops. She looks around for another seat. There's only one other free seat, next to this big black guy, but he's big, so there's not much room. That's where the Mexican mother sits. She has trouble holding her baby in her arms and trying to fold up the stroller, but she manages. This black guy she's sitting next to is about four feet taller than she is. Or at least it seems that way. Mean-looking, too. His arms are thick like telephone poles. He's got this look on his face like he hates everyone, like you better not mess with him."

"Like you guys," says Kevin.

"Exactly. So naturally I stare him down as I walk by, make sure he doesn't look at me. Paco doesn't even notice him because he's checking out some skinny Vietnamese girl with her purse on her lap, probably going to work. And he starts talking to her, but she doesn't say much.

"When I get to the back of the bus, I sit down, and this black guy turns around and looks at me. Hard.

"I thought maybe he's pissed that we didn't give the mother our seats, since we had three of them, one each, and one between us, you know, the faggot buffer zone."

"That's not very nice," says Shelly. "'Fag' is an ugly word."

"You're right," I say. "Gang members aren't politically correct. That's just the way we talked. So this black guy is looking at me."

"African-American," corrects Shelly.

"Like he thought he was bad. His face is all scrunched up like he was challenging me. I had to do something. So I stand up."

"Were you packing?" asks Kevin.

"No, not that day. I walk over to this black guy, and he's looking at me hard the whole time I'm walking over there. I get to where he is and I say, 'You got a problem, dogg?' He says nothing, just stares hard. I notice the baby in the mother's arms is staring up at me, too, his eyes wide open, and he's happy, his little hands and fingers reaching up for me. He's making ga ga noises. I say to the black guy, 'You want to F with me. Let's go, punk!'"

"Damn," says Kevin.

"I don't think I want to hear this," says Mom.

"And that's when it happened. The black dude, man, he fucking smiles at me, a big slobbery smile. And he lifts his hands like he's got no control over the movement. They're bending at the wrists and shit. And he starts making noises with his mouth. Funny noises.

"The young Mexican mother looks up at me. 'Please,' she says, 'Leave him alone.' The black guy jerks his neck, involuntarily, and he says to me, 'Hi, you! Hi!' and he waves again. Then his face goes back to the hard way it was before, only now I see that his eyes are not mean, but innocent. I guess, he was mentally retarded."

I turn to Shelly. "Or however it's called."

I see that the TV is playing a commercial that's supposed to be funny.

I notice the ceiling fan is on low.

The family is silent.

Vern starts. He busts out laughing. I want to tell him that he better watch himself.

He continues laughing with a few "oh mys" and some tears. Shelly can't help it, she laughs too, not at the story but at Vern. She stops laughing and shakes her head at Vern for laughing.

Vern says, wiping tears of laughter from his eyes, "Sorry, man. It's just that. . . That's a great story! Great! You ought to publish it."

"It was very nice," agrees mom.

"Call it 'Retarded Noises!'" says Vern, as if repeating a punch line.

"You better check yourself," I say.

"Seriously, bro. Great story." His face is serious now, dark and sweaty. "Thanks for sharing that, man.

Seriously. It reminds me of something that happened to me. I was at Denny's because I wanted to order the Grand Slam breakfast, but the waiter wouldn't take my order. He was behind the fricken register, talking to some other employee. I walked over to him and I said, 'Hey what the hell's up here? Why aren't you waiting on me? Do you know how long I've been waiting?' And he looked at me and started making retarded noises, 'Doy doy doy,' with a big slobbering smile, and I suddenly realized he was retarded. Man, I felt so bad. Changed my life."

He laughs at his joke.

Under the table my fists are clenched.

"Stop it, Vern," says Shelly, looking at me, concerned about what I might do.

Vern says through laughter, "Oh, and one time, on my way home from work, I got pulled over by a cop. I was really pissed off because I knew I wasn't speeding. I learned my lesson with those other four tickets, believe me, I was not speeding. I was about to tell this cop off. He got to my window and I said, 'What the hell you stopping me for?' But then I noticed he was slobbering. Then — oh, this is so sad — he had this big smile on his face and he was making retarded noises! 'Doy doy doy.' Oh, I felt so guilty!"

I stand up. Vern keeps laughing. The family steps in closer.

"Stop," I say. "You'll regret it."

Vern looks up at me. I can see in his eyes that he knows I'm serious now.

My mother says, "Please, God, no."

I look so deep in his eyes that I think I can see something raging against me. I can hear him breathing, see his nostrils rise and fall. He does not turn away. He stares in my eyes, like he's ready for me. A buzz rings out. We both look away. My mom, smiling nervously, says, "Cookies are ready." With fat mitts she pulls the tray from the womb of the oven and then holds it out so all of us can see. Shelly rises from the couch, Vern perks up. Kevin's wide eyes watch the tray from over mom's shoulder. For a moment we are all silent and still. The cookies sparkle with sugar and are shaped like Christmas trees, little green triangles.

AMERICANO

So if love is possible from a photograph, why was it wrong for Vladimir Cruz to feel love for the boy in the leather pants? After all, his father, a respected man, had fallen in love with a photograph of his mother and had written to her in Cuba promising to come get her, if she would have him. He had gotten off the plane in Havana and saw her standing at the gate in a yellow dress, nervously tugging at the collar, and he knew he had done the right thing. So why did Vladimir feel guilty every time he stood at the window hoping to see the boy in the leather pants coming out of his big white house? Why did he feel like a peeping tom, why not just go downstairs, walk across the street, and introduce himself?

One evening after he took off his gun and set it on the kitchen counter, next to a bottle of wine, he started to cook chicken breasts in garlic and lemon, and as he chopped and prepped, he thought that maybe he felt so guilty because he wasn't really in love. Still, he remembered that image so clearly — as if he himself held a photo — that one time he had seen the boy coming out of the big white house. He was the most beautiful and refreshing person Vladimir had theretofore seen in Marshall, Minnesota, and he could tell by close observation that the boy was gay or bi or was going to be someday. As Vladimir lifted fingers full of chopped garlic and sprinkled the pieces into the hot olive oil — hissing like a secret — he thought that perhaps he was projecting his hatred for his new life in rural Minnesota onto this attachment to the boy.

He added onions, which sizzled, and he moved the pieces of onion and garlic around the pan with a wooden spoon. He squeezed lemon into the hot oil.

His parents knew how to love, but Vladimir was being selfish, childish. He couldn't love the boy in the leather pants; in fact, the fact that he thought of him with that name, "the boy in the leather pants," as if that were his only identity, showed him that the day Vladimir had seen the boy out the window, he had fallen in love with an image, an icon framed by wood, a painting on the wall.

When the chicken breasts were cooked white and moist in the middle, he spooned a bed of orzo onto his plate and laid a breast on it. He grabbed the bottle of wine next to his gun, and he went into the large dining room, almost empty. He sat next to the window at the little table, which reflected on the shiny wood floors, the blur of his reflection like a silent movie. He looked out into the sun as he ate, at the boy's big white house surrounded by oak trees.

The Somali lady led Vladimir into her dark living room. The curtains were drawn and the smell of coffee beans and melting butter came from the kitchen. She sat on her couch and Vladimir sat across from her on an armchair. She slowly lifted her long, black fingers to her hair and said, "He beats me." She pulled the collar of her *guntiino*, a white sari-like dress, and showed him the bruises on her neck. Then she pulled the garment up her sleeve and revealed the purple blotches on her arm.

"Can I have him arrested?" she asked.

"Of course. He has no right to hit you," Vladimir said.

"It isn't allowed by your government?" she asked.

"I guess you could put it that way."

She picked up her naked baby from the carpet and held it in her arms, the baby's fingers grasping for her neck as he stared with big eyes at Vladimir. Then the baby made sounds, as if he were trying to talk, saliva clinging to his bottom lip. Vladimir smiled and the baby laughed. The mother pulled her head away to look at the face of her child, and seeing how happy he looked, she laughed too.

The husband was standing in the apartment parking lot smoking cigarettes with three other Somali men, all of them dressed in Western clothes that seemed to be from the 1970s, bellbottom jeans, long-sleeved shirts. These dark black men stood out against the horizon of cornfields and beyond that the sloping prairie of tall grass. The rhythm of their native language reminded him of drums and flutes, but they were suddenly silent when they noticed him approach. They continued to smoke, blowing white clouds right at the stranger, as if in disdain. "I'm looking for Madoowbee," he said, pulling out his wallet and flashing the flashy badge. All four men ran, disappearing behind walls and garbage dumpsters. Vladimir ran after Madoowbee, yelling that he just wanted to talk, but the husband shot across the street and into a cornfield. Vladimir could see his head slide across the top of the crop, but he didn't bother to chase him any further because Marshall was small, about 12,000 people, and most of the Somalis worked at the turkey plant. There was no place to hide. At the edge of the cornfield, the Somali reached the old cemetery, dark under the oak trees, and he vanished into a row of tombstones.

Later that afternoon, Vladimir was on another call. He sat in the jailhouse and watched a guard lead a handcuffed Mexican man down the cement hallway. He had been arrested for statutory rape, but Jeremy, the DA, wanted to elevate the charges to child molestation. Jeremy wanted the Mexican to get time. "He doesn't speak English, so you have to find out what you can, take his statement."

Now, the Mexican sat across from Vladimir, hands cuffed behind his back. His eyes looked around, a frightened man trying not to look frightened.

"Are you O.K.?" Vladimir asked him in Spanish.

"Where did you learn Spanish?" the Mexican asked.

"I'm Cuban," Vladimir said.

"Why are you in Minnesota?"

"Just like you," he said. "For the work."

"You don't kill turkeys."

"No, you're right," said Vladimir.

"Are you here to help?"

"Well…"

The Mexican's eyes were big and brown like in a Diego Rivera painting.

"Truth is," Vladimir said, "I want a statement about your relationship to…" He had to look down on the file to remember her name. "Amber Tholen." He looked up. "I'm with the DA. Everything you say is for the record, and if you don't want to talk, you don't have to. I represent the DA. He's the one who wants to prosecute."

"I'm in love with Amber," he said. "We want to get married. Her parents don't like me, because I'm Mexican."

"How old is she?"

"Fourteen."

"What's the age difference between you two?"
"Four years."

Outside the jail, the girl came up to Vladimir in tears. She was a large girl with bleached blonde hair and she smelled of hairspray and cigarettes. She said she loved Miguel. She held Vladimir's elbow. "Please don't let nothing happen to him."

At night, as he cooked vegetable curry, he thought about the boy in the leather pants. He looked down into the bubbling clay pot scented of coconut milk and curry and thought that perhaps he appealed to him because of some spiritual connection, something beyond logic. When he thought of him, as he often did, he didn't think of him sexually. He didn't picture him walking across the room naked, stepping out of his pants or coming up behind him while he cooked, putting his arms around him, kissing his neck, pulling up his shirt and kissing his back, pressing his body against his. He didn't picture him coming to bed, or lying next to him, or kissing him, and he didn't think of the boy's wet mouth, saliva like fresh spring water. He was prepared to believe it was true love, but then he felt himself getting an erection, so he shook those thoughts from his mind, and he pulled a plate from the cupboard.

He told himself, "See? It's not love, it's lust." And he poured a ladle of curry over a bed of white, steamed rice.

He was lonely. He hated Marshall. There wasn't a single person in town that he could call right now and say, "Please, come over for some curry." There was no one to call and have a beer with. The rural Midwestern culture seemed to him cold, and at the same time he acknowledged that he wasn't the easiest guy to get along with. He knew that he could come across as arrogant. One time he had heard one of the lawyers on the phone saying, "I don't think he likes white people," and he assumed that they were talking about him. And maybe it seemed that way, he had to admit. There was a certain amount of superiority he felt, being from Miami, an international city, a thriving city. He had at least seen a bit of the world, whereas most of these rural people rarely left town. For them to get away meant to drive three hours to the Twin Cities and shop at the Mall of America.

Yes, he could be a snob, and quite frankly, he couldn't think of one person in the DA's office that he would *want* to call and say, "Please, come over and have some curry."

The next day as he drove down Main Street he saw the boy walking into a bank with a bouquet of roses in his arms. The boy's beauty pricked him so painfully that he pulled to the side of the road, and, feeling somewhat perverse, waited for the boy to come back out. His white van was parked on the street and he noticed for the first time that the side of the van said "Hyvee Florist. Free Delivery."

"He delivers flowers," he said out loud. He waited to see him walk out again. When the boy did walk out, Vladimir sunk in his seat so he wouldn't be seen. The boy wore jeans and a black T-shirt. He walked with a bounce, as if life were great. He jumped into his van and took off. Vladimir rose in his seat and watched the van get smaller as it went down the road. Suddenly he heard a knock on his glass and he jumped. On the passenger's side a face appeared.

The lady framed by the window had a big smile and pale blue eyes.

"Hiya!" she said. "Whatcha doing out here?"

"Name's Nora. That's mine," she said, pointing to the cafe he was parked in front of, a wooden sign reading "Higher Ground."

He apologized for parking there, but she said, "No, no. I wanted to invite you in for a cappuccino. On the house."

"What do you mean?"

"You're new to town, aren't you? You work with Jeremy, the DA. You're Vladimir, right?"

He said that he was Vladimir, thanked her, but said that he was in a hurry.

"No, no," she said, walking around the car, to his door and opening it. "One cup. Out. Out."

"Er, thanks."

She must have been in her mid-thirties to early forties, light brown hair, blue eyes, thin, and pretty in a plain sort of way. He could picture her as a hippie. Unconsciously, he calculated what must have been the age difference between them, him 27, and her at maybe 40, maybe 38. He decided on 38. Eleven years' difference. She dressed normally, he thought, like anyone he would see in Miami or any other US city, tight jeans, sleeveless top, navy blue tennis shoes. She didn't look like rural Minnesota, but she had the accent. "You'll love my cappuccino," she said, as she stood behind the bar getting ready to make whatever he wanted. "Wanna try it?"

The place smelled of freshly-ground coffee beans.

Lining the shelves behind the bar were jars of roasted beans.

"I'll just take a regular cup of coffee," he said.

"How about an Americano?" she said.

"Sure," he said, and he sat at a table. As she stood before the espresso machine, she said over the hiss of the steamy water, "You know what they call an Americano in France?"

"No I don't."

"*Café allongé.* I've always wondered why."

"Because it's water added to espresso and thus it's elongated?" He shrugged his shoulders.

She turned around to look at him. "Sounds right to me."

"Just guessing."

"You could be right."

"It smells good in here," he said. "I appreciate good coffee. It's good to know someone in town has some. I thought I'd have to drive to the Twin Cities every time I ran out of beans."

"I have the beans sent fresh from the roaster every two weeks."

A bookshelf against one of the walls held hardbound copies of classics, *War and Peace, A Tale of Two Cities, Parallel Lives.*

"How many times have you been to France?" he asked.

"A few," she said. She put the coffee before him and sat down. Many things about her looked so young, her smooth hair, the way she dressed, her slender figure, but the flesh on her arm wiggled as she absentmindedly twisted a yellow cloth napkin and watched him take the first sip.

"So? How do you like our town?" she asked.

"Doesn't seem like there's much to do for a single person," he said.

"Yeah, that's true," she said, raising her eyebrows, as if he were saying the obvious. "Wake up and smell the prairie, Vlad."

"Wake up and smell the homogeneity," he said.

"Smell the night."

"The night?" he asked.

"Lonely rural nights," she said.

"You got that right," he said.

"You hate it here," she said. "And who can blame you? Jeremy says you're from Miami." She fiddled with the napkin, and then, with very little enthusiasm, she said, "Ta da!" and placed the napkin on the table. She had folded it into a yellow rose.

"Great," he said.

She unfurled the napkin and looked out the window, the crow's feet coming from her eyes. "I got a million of 'em," she said. She tilted her head and slightly smiled, as if, in the distance, she heard a song she thought she recognized.

At the turkey plant, Vladimir came up behind Madoowbee, but the man didn't try to run. "You got me," he said as he continued to cut the guts off the birds.

"I just want to talk."

"My wife, my business."

Vladimir didn't try to argue. He just asked questions about what happened and wrote down the answers. The plant stunk of blood and wet feathers. Vladimir's own father had once worked in a fishery, and as a child Vladimir was sometimes led by his mom into the mouth of the great slippery building, holding her hand with one hand and plugging his nose with the other.

As he listened to the Somali man talk, he thought about his gentle father, how one time he had gotten so angry at his mother that he said something mean and left the house for a few hours. But he had never hit her. He wondered what brought this man to see it as acceptable and what brought his wife, thankfully, to see that it was not. Vladimir didn't know, and he felt slightly sad to know that it wasn't his job to know. He worked for the prosecutor.

On his way out of the turkey plant, the wife came out of the work area and followed him down the brick hallway. She told him that she had changed her mind. She didn't want to press charges. "Are you sure?" he asked. She said yes, but as he walked out, she said, "Mister?" and he turned around. She stood framed by the square of the cement hallway, and behind her the shadows of turkeys slid by, hanging upside down on shackles. "I can change my mind sometime?"

"Anytime you want," he said.

At the office, Vladimir wrote up his report. The DA and a few other lawyers were laughing as they put on their coats to go have a drink. The DA asked if Vladimir wanted to join them at the Wooden Nickel. Vladimir thanked him, but said he had work to do, and when they left, the office was quiet. He pulled the Marshall phonebook from his desk drawer, and he looked up florists. There were only two in town. He picked up the phone and dialed Hyvee's. He ordered a dozen white flowers to be delivered to his home.

He went home, took a shower, and cooked shrimp scampi, which scented the room long after he had eaten. He didn't eat much, however, because he was nervous. He had a few glasses of wine at the tiny eating table next to the window.

He waited.

He drank a third and then a fourth glass of wine.

Finally, the doorbell rang and he answered it.

He stood up, nervous, and he walked to the door.

The boy stood at the threshold holding the flowers. He wore jeans and a tight T-shirt that said, "GUESS" across the chest.

"You Vladimir?" he asked.

"Vladimir Cruz."

"Got your flowers," the boy said.

"Come on in," he said

He asked the boy to put them on the eating table, and as he bent over to set them down, Vladimir looked out the window. The boy's white house shone in the middle of the window, like a painting he had meant to take down. The boy looked out. "That's my house," he said.

"Oh, really?" Vladimir said, feeling as if he had been caught looking through the boy's window. "I'm new to Marshall."

"Duh," the boy said, looking him up and down, hands on his hips.

Vladimir looked at the "G" and the "S" across the boy's chest, and then he looked away.

"Is it that obvious that I'm new?" he said.

"Well, there's not very many cute guys around here." The boy paused to see what Vladimir's reaction would be. "You're not shocked."

"Not surprised."

"Everyone's in the closet here," said the boy. "But I could tell with you," he says. "I've noticed you. There's not many black guys in Marshall. Except for those Somalis, but I mean cool guys. They're. . . you know, *African* African."

"*African* African?"

"You know. They're not Americans."

"Would you like to have a seat?" he said, indicating a chair at the little eating table.

"Sure, why not?" The boy sat.

Vladimir sat.

Between them was the window, the big white house lit up like a Thomas Kincaid painting.

The boy looked around Vladimir's place, the empty dining room, and then into his narrow kitchen. "You have a gun," he said, perking up, as if he wanted to get up and handle it. "You a cop?"

"I work for the DA," he said. "An investigator. Would you like a glass of wine?"

"Can't," he said.

"Oh, yeah, you're driving. Sorry."

"Yeah, if I got fired, my parents would kill me."

"Your parents?"

"Yup. So where are you from?"

"Miami," he said.

"Vladimir's a funny name for a black guy," the boy said.

"I'm Cuban."

"Really? Like that Elian boy?"

"Kind of," he said.

"I like black guys," the boy said.

He wasn't sure if he was supposed to thank him. "You still live with your parents?" he said. "Is that a rural Minnesota thing?"

"No, it's a still in high school and being sixteen thing."

"High school?" He took a drink of his wine.

"Yup. How old are you?"

After the boy left, Vladimir opened all the windows to let in the cold wind, because he felt his face burning. He sat near the window. The flowers he had ordered looked like an unwanted baby on the table, facing him. In the cold wind, he could smell the burnt corn from the processing plant, and he could smell the wet feathers of the turkey plant. He could hear the leaves of the oak trees around the white house softly laughing in the breeze. He pictured the Somalis and Mexicans working together, he pictured Miguel and Madoowbee working side by side, trading jokes with the gestures of their hands and exaggerated expressions on their faces. He could smell the wet dirt in the flowerpot in front of his face. He smelled stale wine coming from his glass.

Then, as clear as anything had ever been, he realized what he needed, what he wanted more than anything. He stood up, ran to his bedroom closet and pulled out a light coat with the Nike logo on the chest. He put it on, and without cleaning up, without grabbing his gun, without even locking the front door, he ran down the stairs of his apartment building, to the street, got in his car, and drove as fast as he could to the "Higher Ground" for a strong cup of Americano.

THE CRAZY CHICKEN

My mother saw herself in the mirror, her face sunken from not eating. She was lying on her hospice bed in the middle of our living room. "I look pretty bad," she said, touching what was left of her hair, as if all she had to do was arrange it and she could grab her keys, go out of the house and have a regular day. My brother Bobby stepped in front of the mirror, covering her image, a tall and heavy man. He took her hand and said, "You're beautiful as ever."

"Don't say that," she said. Then she ran out of energy and plopped her head back on the pillow, closed her eyes.

I was sitting on an armchair editing a story I had just written. I was a new writer, or suddenly thought that I might become one. My very first story was going to be work-shopped by the creative writing class that evening. I was pretty proud of it, my first ever, and I was sure that the people in the workshop would like it. I couldn't help but reread it, over and over. *Who was this chicken? Some giant bird from Mexican folklore that came out at night and endowed good boys and girls, the ones who obeyed their parents, with intelligence and ambition?*

The story was about a Chicano boy, a young man my age, who, like me, didn't really fit in with the Chicanos and didn't fit in with the whites either. One day, he was attending the Chicano graduation ceremony at the university, because he was graduating with a B.A. in Political Science, like me, and like me he didn't know what he would do next.

He (my character) didn't speak Spanish, and when some of the students took the stage and said their speeches in Spanish, he could have sworn that he heard many of them thanking the *Pollo Loco*. What they were really saying (unknown to him) was something like *gracias por su apoyo, lo que me ayudó*, but he only heard the **poyo lo que**, which he thought was *Pollo Loco*. He knew some Spanish words, not a lot, only what his mother had taught him when he was growing up, things like mi'jo and ven acá y te quiero y vámanos y porfavor ¡no me dejes solo! — he knew enough Spanish to know that Pollo Loco meant Crazy Chicken. As he heard some of the graduates who spoke Spanish thanking the Crazy Chicken, he suddenly felt as if he had been left out of a great source of power that everyone else had but him. It was a source of magic from Mexican lore, this Crazy Chicken, this chicken who helped so many young Mexicans, but never him, because he didn't speak Spanish.

Now, it was too late.

I looked up from my story and across the dimly-lit living room. I could see in the mirror. It had a gold-colored frame like an old painting. I saw myself sitting on the chair. I saw Bobby standing before my mother's death bed. Red pillows. I saw my mother's head slowly move, and then she moaned.

"She's in pain," said my sister Betty. She was standing in the doorframe to the kitchen. "We should give her more medicine."

"Let's wait," said Bobby. "She's sleeping. When she wakes."

"You guys want to hear my story?" I said.

They both looked at me. My mother lightly moaned, like she was having a bad dream (Surprise, Mom! Wake up

Mexico to find an after hours club. We dance all night. When the place closes, we're still not satisfied. We stand by the car, the sun already shining, the desert mountains lit up.

When we get home, I take off my clothes. I forget to take off my Texas Ranger cowboy hat. Walking down the hallway to the shower, I see myself in the full-length mirror, naked, with my cowboy hat still on. "Howdy, pardner," I say to myself.

I suddenly remember my sixth birthday party. I remember flashes from the camera and my father walking toward me on his knees, clicking photo after photo. I remember our little kitchen table was scattered with Tupperware glasses of Kool-Aid and a half-eaten white cake.

I remember that my parents got me a cowboy hat and holster and sheriff's badge. I played cowboy all day. After the neighborhood kids left, my mom told me to take a bath, but I didn't want to quit playing cowboy. I got naked, but I didn't take off my holster and hat. In the photo that still exists, I'm naked, running through the house, shooting my cap gun into the air, my little penis vibrating like stubby rubber.

My mom crooned, "How cute!" her hands on her cheeks, and my older brothers and sisters were laughing.

The camera flashes.

I see myself naked with my Texas Ranger cowboy hat in the full-length mirror. I'm a tall man, six-three, but I feel like a child. An idea comes to me. I giggle as I tiptoe to get my toy gun on the nightstand next to the bed. I hold the handle firmly and run into the living room.

Marisol sits on the couch reading something on the screen of her laptop, perhaps another email from Guatemala.

She has been getting a lot of emails from home, or maybe she just re-reads the one she got last week from her sister telling her about it. This must be the fourth or fifth time she has read it, or at least that I've seen her read it. Once she read it to me, but she read so fast, her voice cracking with so much emotion, that I just listened to the sweet, sad sound of it. I lost track of the meaning. It was in Spanish, and I was too embarrassed to tell her I didn't get it the first time. All I know is that it has to do with home, something about her town, and that it isn't good, and that there isn't anything she can do about it.

I jump in front of her.

It dangles.

"This is the police!" I yell.

I run around the house shooting my toy gun, yelling, "Bang bang! You're dead!"

I run through the dining room, into the kitchen, into the library, through Marisol's office, where I flick on the lights so I don't trip over her map-tables and globes. On the wall above her computer hangs a map of the Americas. All over her desk are articles and tapes about the Juarez women, her dissertation research.

I run out of her office and back into the living room. I expect her to be giggling, maybe looking for the camera so she can take a shot, maybe yelling things like, "Oh, honey, that's so cute!"

Instead, I see that she's still reading the letter. Her indigenous face is still as stone.

"Hey, you're under arrest," I say.

She slowly raises her head to look at me, the blue screen of the laptop glowing on her chin. "You can't," she says. "You can't."

EL REGALITO

The tourist wore short khaki pants and hiking boots, white socks pulled up almost to his knees, and a backpack strapped over both shoulders like a boy going to school. He was a white man, haggling with an old street vendor, who sold crosses from the baskets on his bicycle. He told the tourist he had carved and painted them himself, with the help of his little girl.

"Cincuenta pesos," said the old man.

"Te doy veinte," said the tourist.

The old vendor held his wooden cross to his chest and shook his head. "Veinte? No, no puedo. Cuarenta sí." He wore a straw hat frayed at the edges.

The tourist could smell hot, steaming corn from the vendor next to them, a big lady in a red hat, and it made him sort of nauseous. He looked at his watch. He never ate on the street, because he couldn't know if it was safe, and he was on his way to some priest's birthday party on another side of town. He had been invited by the lady who rented him a room.

She had said it was a neighborhood party in the barrio San Antón, and that there would be "nice" girls there, not like the kind he would meet at a disco. She said La Ruta #122, which he could catch in the zócalo, would take him right to the doors of the church.

The zócalo vibrated with life, families, young lovers, street vendors, men walking around with guitars, mariachis standing on street corners waiting to be hired. Children ran all over the place like demons, chasing each other, running up and down the stairs of the gazebo in the middle of the plaza. Potbellied men with black shoes sat on shoeshine chairs reading magazines they had bought from the newsstands behind them, where the newspapers were stacked so high they reached higher than the heads of the old men who bent over to shine the shoes. Laughter and music came from all sides, and the trees were filled with thousands of birds, violently screeching. A group of Goth-looking teenagers in black leather and white makeup were hanging around a bench, laughing and talking, and the tourist shook his head, as if he were disappointed in those Mexican kids, because he felt they were taking away the authenticity of their own traditional zócolo.

He saw #122 coming toward the plaza, and knowing he had no time for foolishness, he turned around and said to the old man, "Veinte. Nada más. It's a gift for a priest," he said. "It's his birthday. Un regalito para el sacerdote," he said.

The old vendor shook his head, not in disdain, or to say "no" to the tourist, but in resignation, as if he knew he had no other choice. He looked at his bicycle wheel, and his young daughter was peeking at him through the spokes, the tire taller than her. She was about six years old, her big brown eyes looking back and forth at her father and the tourist. Reluctantly, the old man agreed on 35.

The tourist handed him a 50-peso note and asked for change. The vendor — like he had all the time in the world — pulled from his front basket a plastic bag. He put the cross inside and twisted it closed, the bag spinning around and around like an orb. He handed the bag to the tourist.

Number 122 reached the plaza, opened its doors and released its heavy sigh.

"¡Mi cambio, ándale!" he said.

The old man, again as if he had all the time in the world, stuck his hand into his pant pocket. He pulled out a leather change-purse, flaking with age. He pulled down the zipper and counted the white man's coins.

The tourist, certain the old man was delaying him on purpose, tried to contain his annoyance, his face swelling and turning red, as if he were holding his breath. "¡Andale! ¡Andale!" he said. He snapped his fingers. "¡Arriba! ¡Arriba!"

It just so happened that the tourist, after receiving his coins, ran through the plaza to the sidewalk.

"¡Para para!" he yelled at the bus, which was barely starting to move. The bus driver didn't stop, even though he saw the tourist through the still-open door. He smiled evilly at the white man, and laughed. The tourist cursed and cursed like a teenager. He was not only angry with the street vendor and the bus driver, but he was also angry with Mexico.

A high school Spanish teacher from Wisconsin, the tourist had come to Cuernavaca to improve his fluency at a language school. He'd been there for two months and hated so much about the country, like the dirty public bathrooms which rarely had soap and hot water. He hated that Mexicans removed the toilet seats so you couldn't sit down and how they put soiled tissue in a waste-paper baskets next to the commode. He hated how no one seemed to be in a hurry. They took forever to bring him his coffee or to give him his bill in a restaurant. What he hated most, however, was the thought of going back to Wisconsin. His hatred for Mexico was sentimental, like a kid praying, "Kill her, God. Kill her," after being punished by his mother. Truth was, he loved Mexico.

He had planned to stay for three weeks, because his

Spanish was good enough, but when he arrived and found out how nice the people were, how every day the weather was beautiful in Cuernavaca, and how cheaply he could live, he changed his plane ticket and decided to stay until the end of the summer.

Now he hated that he had missed the bus. He walked around the plaza, mumbling curses under his breath. He looked mean and unapproachable, like a Nazi officer in a rage, and he didn't notice that people got out of his way. He was tall and thin, and he wore wire-framed eyeglasses like a professor. He walked quickly around the plaza, waiting for the next bus, the plastic bag grasped in his fingers. His hands were huge. He sat on a bench, next to a family eating corn from a Styrofoam cup. That nauseous smell upped his anger. He slapped a hand on his knee and got up again. He was slightly balding and had a long nose and a face that was scrunched up as if he were perpetually angry.

He knew that the busses came by every ten or fifteen minutes, but still he felt like a victim, because he only had two more weeks left in Cuernavaca and he didn't want to waste any time getting what he was hoping to get in Mexico. Although he wouldn't have admitted it to himself or put it in so many words, he didn't want to go back to Wisconsin without a wife.

Back home, he had little luck with women. Even the two single secretaries at the school wouldn't go out with him. They mostly ignored him, and when they did have to speak with him, they made sure they called him Mr. Most girls considered him ugly. He didn't consider himself ugly. He thought of himself as intelligent and scholarly looking, but he feared that the older he got (he was now 36) the more unlikely it was that he would marry an American woman. In Wisconsin, women were rude to him. It made him angry that they seemed to think that he was checking them out whenever they walked by, which, in fact, he was. But still. He wasn't a player who wanted several sex partners, just one good, beautiful intelligent woman.

In Mexico beautiful women talked to him all the time. They smiled and asked him questions and invited him to parties and dances. At first he was suspicious of everyone, figuring that all they wanted in inviting him was a gringo sucker, that maybe their boyfriends would be waiting in dark alleys to rob him. One girl he went out with asked if she could borrow a few pesos to make a phone call, and as she walked toward the phone, he felt used and angry, his pockets lighter. He wondered what she would ask for next, but later that afternoon when she paid him back, he felt so bad that he insisted she keep it, to which she shook her head and handed him the money. They never asked for anything from him, and the more he got to realize that some people were just nice, he felt bad for ever having doubted. He felt racist. He felt white.

Mexican people were good people.

He could spend hours in the zócalo watching the girls walk by, listening to the click of their high heels on the cement, some so heartbreakingly beautiful he felt depressed knowing he would never know them.

"Fuck that bus driver," he thought.

This tourist didn't really understand Mexico, but he didn't know that he didn't understand Mexico. He didn't know that missing the bus was a gift from the universe, if he could only see it that way. He didn't know that if he would have gotten on la Ruta #122, like he had wanted to, he would have never made it to the priest's party.

That smiling bus driver who kept going, even though he knew the tourist was running to catch the bus, might have been an angel, because had the tourist gotten on that bus, here's what would have happened.

He would have handed five pesos to the driver (the change from the hands of the old vendor), a young, dark kid who had a tiny body and long hair. The bus driver, like a pre-teenager, would have had to reach out his skinny arms to grab both sides of the steering wheel. Strapped onto the dashboard with a bungee cord, a boom box blasted Mexican rock. Inside the bus was very loud and hot. The tourist got his change from the boy, counted it to make sure, and then he turned around to take a seat. The bus was almost full. His only choices were to remain standing until someone got off, hanging on to one of those metal rails on top, or he could sit next to a pretty girl on her way home from work at a shoe store. What he would choose of these two would have different consequences, which would then split off into worlds with other, multiple possibilities, other paths that the tourist would never see.

On the rickety Ruta #122, the pretty shoe salesgirl was sitting next to the window looking out. The tourist felt like she was the only one on the bus not staring at him, because everyone else watched him, maybe, he thought, because they were surprised to see a gringo on la Ruta. The tourist, still standing in the bus as it moved along its route, looked at the girl. She was wearing a white blouse and tight red skirt. His memory of loneliness was activated and he suddenly felt sad. He felt worthless, unlovable. Everyone in the bus was looking at him, hating him, resentful to him that he was riding with them on *their* bus. He chose to sit next to the girl.

He thought that if he were a different man he would have started up a conversation with her, but today his Spanish felt hard and heavy and he was afraid he'd seem like an average gringo. He wanted her to know that he really loved Mexico and that he was, in many ways, a Mexican trapped in a gringo's body. But he remembered what rejection felt like, it hurt, so he said nothing. Instead, he just surreptitiously looked at her. He felt wounded by her hair, long, black, and shiny. His energy was so dark, so depressed, that the girl began to feel uncomfortable, especially knowing she was under his glare. She pulled at the sleeve of her blouse, touched her ear, and looked out the window. She saw that on the roof of a crumbling building, a dog barked at passersby.

He didn't notice her discomfort because he was giving off too much of his own. He thought she was exactly what he needed in his life, a woman like her. He imagined she was hardworking, a good girl who went to Mass.

He wanted her.

He noticed how her eyelashes twitched and how her eyes were big and black. He didn't notice how she tried to look at him, without moving her head, through the corner of her eyes, to see if he was still looking. She felt very uncomfortable, as if he were undressing her in his mind.

The beauty mark on her neck, a tiny black dot, turned him on. He noticed, too, how the white straps of her bra were showing through the sheer fabric of her white blouse. He noticed that her skirt rose up to the middle of her thighs and that even though she was not wearing pantyhose, her legs were smooth and without blemish. He noticed her smell. He didn't notice how he was leaning in a little closer to take a whiff, which caused her to clutch her purse more tightly on her lap.

He was prepared at anytime, should she look over at him, to pretend to be looking past her, out the window to the street. Twilight was becoming night. He would pretend to be fascinated by the storefront businesses, the taquerías, the bright white pharmacies, dark windows in stone buildings. He saw three teenage boys sitting in a well-lit restaurant without walls. The boy in the middle, at the exact moment that the tourist looked, took a drink from a bottle of apple soda.

The tourist remembered apples.

When he was a child he had gone to visit his aunt in Oregon. She had lived alone in a big white house on a street with other big houses, many converted into apartments. His aunt was old and couldn't maintain her house, so tall grass and weeds covered the front yard. There were seven apple trees around the house, and after they ripened into plump green orbs, the apples fell to the ground and rotted and opened and sprayed a sweet fragrance through the window at night while he tried to sleep. Like syrup. He loved it so much he would never eat an apple. They were gross to look at, fleshy guts spilling from the slits with worms, smashed all over the yard and sidewalk. But he loved the smell. He remembered the smell now on la Ruta #122 in Cuernavaca.

In Wisconsin the high school Spanish teacher lived alone in a one-bedroom apartment on the third floor. It was always dark, because there were no windows except for one that looked across at the neighbor's wall. Inside he felt imprisoned, but he couldn't afford anything else and didn't have the will to move. He never had anyone over his place, and when the phone rang, he jumped up from his seat or from where he lay on his bed as if that sound were a cry of hope. He hoped that each phone call was someone inviting him out, but it was usually a telemarketer or a prank call from a student he had flunked. On weekends, if it wasn't too cold, he walked to a local pub, a place called the Wounded Knee, and he had two beers. As he sat at the bar, he furtively watched the people, pretending to be too occupied with deep thoughts to notice anyone. He hoped that some woman would notice him, would come up to him and say, "Wow, you must really be thinking about something important. I've been trying to get your attention all night." When he went home alone, he turned on the TV, walked back and forth in the living room. "You're ugly," he'd say. "No woman will ever want you."

He felt those feelings of failure now. He wasn't good enough for the pretty shoe salesgirl, or for any woman. What a fool he was to pretend he had a chance with the girls in Mexico. They were nice, and maybe at first they really cared about him, but not one girl would kiss him. He tried with one, and she stepped back, shook "no" with her finger and said, "No soy norte americana."

So much was he collapsing under the gravity of his own depression that he missed his bus stop. He didn't notice when the bus passed right by the church in barrio San Antón, and by the time he realized his mistake, he was in an unfamiliar neighborhood. The sidewalks were crumbling here, gang graffiti painted all over the walls. Here, on the dark street, he saw a group of men, boys really, standing around an old beat up American car, drinking beer. The tourist, blonde-haired, blue-eyed, knew that he stood out in places where there were no tourists. He believed that the boys drinking beer by the car saw into the passing bus and noticed him. He got nervous. They would be waiting for him at the next stop. He grabbed the metal rail on the seat in front of him and looked around the neighborhood, hoping to see even one gringo.

Unconsciously, the tourist evaluated his sense of security in Mexico by how many other gringos he saw.

If there were a lot, he felt too safe, as if he wasn't really experiencing Mexico, but if there were only a few tourists here and there, he not only felt safe, but he felt as if he were seeing authentic Mexico. He liked to experience Mexico in a way that few gringos could. This was why he took la Ruta and not a cab, because on it were *real* Mexicans (authentic Mexican beings) and only an occasional tourist. But if he were in a place where gringos never went, he would feel unsafe.

So, seeing no gringos in this neighborhood, he got nervous that he had gone into a part of Cuernavaca where Americans weren't welcome. He stood up from his seat and walked down the aisle to the front of the bus. He asked the bus driver where they were and how he could get to the church in barrio San Antón. He didn't notice that he had left the bag with the priest's gift on the seat next to the salesgirl.

The bus driver answered him in fast mumbled Spanish that the tourist didn't understand. He didn't want to let on that he didn't understand, because he thought that would make him look too vulnerable, like he didn't know Mexico, so he decided to get off the bus and take a taxi back to the church. At the next stop he got off, and figuring that he needed to go in the opposite direction to get to the church, he crossed the street.

Inside of la Ruta, the shoe salesgirl noticed the bag the tourist had left on the seat. And even though he had made her feel uncomfortable by looking at her so lecherously, even though he deserved to have it hurled away, this young woman yelled out the window, "Señor, Señor, dejó su bolsa."

But lucky for him the tourist missed that bus. He waited in the plaza for the next Ruta #122, and although at first he was impatient waiting, something happened that would change things forever.

It was a story he would tell his future kids, like all stories, with some exaggeration. His kids would sit around the table and listen to their father tell it, and no matter how many times he told them the story, they never tired of it. When they grew up and had kids, they too told the story. Of course, memory is a conduit of feeling, not fact, and some of them would confuse or forget or add some of the details. One son would say it took place in Mexico City while his father was waiting for the metro, and another son would say that it took place in Tijuana while his father was waiting for "el burro." But all of them would agree that it was a good thing that their father missed the first Ruta (or metro or burro).

As he was waiting for the next 122, he looked across the zócalo and saw the old man who had sold him the cross. The man was standing in front of a vendor of elotes, a big lady in a red hat. He was holding his daughter's hand.

The little girl looked excited as she looked up at the gleaming yellow corncob on a stick, on which the lady was spreading thick mayonnaise. Then she sprinkled on chili powder. The little girl rubbed her hands together, as if she were so excited. The old man took the corn on a stick and handed it to his daughter, who had a big, happy smile on her face. Then, for some reason, he looked up, as if he knew he was being watched. He looked right at the tourist. He smiled.

The tourist smiled back.

The old man waved.

The tourist waved back.

The old man turned and watched the vendor prepare his corn.

It occurred to the tourist as he watched them that the little girl may not have been the old man's daughter, more like a granddaughter, because she was so young and he was so old. Or maybe, the tourist considered, he just looked older than his years, because of his days under the sun, peddling his bicycle across cobblestone streets, through plazas and across busy intersections, the crosses in the back baskets rattling in their cages, selling on the streets to tourists all hours, as they stepped out of coffee shops, as they stepped out of bars.

The old Schwinn now leaned against his hip as he stuck his fingers into his coin purse. He pulled out a large coin, a ten-peso piece, but before he could hand it to the elote vendor, the coin slipped from his unsteady fingers. When it hit the ground, it landed on its edge and began to roll across the cement and through the legs of people.

The old man went after his coin, his arms out, like he was trying to catch an injured bird that was hopping away. The coin continued to roll and the man followed it, eyes wide, mouth open like an "O." The tourist laughed.

The coin kept rolling away, like in a comedy, as if it had its own life and it was in a hurry. The old man zigzagged through the people, trying to catch up to it. The tourist laughed, but then it rolled into a circle of Goth-looking teenagers. The old man made his way through them, and he lost sight of it. He kept looking around the legs of people, desperately, although it was obvious he would not find it. The teenagers spread themselves out, out of his way, half-helped him look, but nothing. The old man finally gave up. He walked back to his bike, which he had laid on the ground next to his daughter and the elote cart.

The tourist heard a horn. He turned around and saw that another #122 was pulling up to the plaza. The tourist stuck his hand in his pocket for a coin, and he felt the ten peso piece.

He turned around and saw the man walking. He felt the ten peso coin, and decided that he would tell the old man a lie. *I was just standing around*, he'd tell him, *when all of a sudden a ten-peso coin rolled right by me.*

The tourist didn't catch that bus either, or the next one, and later on that night at the church in the barrio San Antón, he couldn't forget the way the old man smiled when he accepted the coin. His wrinkled face, his bright eyes, his rotting teeth were the most beautiful things he had ever seen. The little girl giggled when the old man showed her the runaway coin.

The birthday party was held outside of the church. They had set up tables and there were streamers and music and everyone was eating. Later that night, some people he had met at the party all went out together, to a disco, to the disco called Freedom. That was where he met Blanca.

"¡Señor! Dejó tu bolsa."

The tourist, crossing the street to catch a taxi, heard a girl call his name. He saw her leaning out of the bus and something wilted within him. She made such a beautiful picture framed by the window. His heart was breaking for this beautiful girl who called for him. Maybe, he thought, in that short time sitting next to him, she saw something special in him. He didn't see the taxi speeding along at 80 kilometers per hour, nor did the cab driver see him. The girl saw it and screamed.

She took his bag home, but feeling so bad, she never looked inside. That night she didn't go out clubbing with her girlfriends to the disco called Freedom, like she had planned, because she couldn't forget the way he died right in front of her eyes. Eventually, the cross ended up in her closet. After she died a very old woman, her grandchildren were cleaning out her house. They found a bag. Inside, they found a wooden cross, painted colorfully with a countryside, peasants working the land, sheep grazing, fishes swimming around a pond.

Even today la Ruta # 122 chugs around the city of Cuernavaca. You can see the number painted on the hood and on both sides of the bus, a white circle with the 122 inside of it. A lot of people don't know that the number of the bus is also painted on the top, on the roof, where only birds and people looking out from balconies can see it. From high above the city, when birds look down on the salad bowl of Cuernavaca, they can see countless busses with the number 122 slithering through the winding streets of the city. The numbers slide through intersections, crisscrossing and slipping past a string of other busses, 9, 11, 3, 7, integers moving around like a bizarro abacus, 23, 14, 17, slithering around, 55, 28, 66, and around. If you pull your view even further away from the earth, they'll look like amoebas floating under the view of a microscope. Further still and you wouldn't be able to detect them vibrating within the topography of Mexico and over the blue curve of earth. You wouldn't be able to discern Cuernavaca and its streets. From up there, the city busses and the units of heat that go in and out of the doors of these busses are unseen energy, particles that twist and turn and interact with others particles and become part of a wave. There are a countless number of these waves ebbing and flowing within the chaos and synchronicity of the cosmos. Together they create time, a formless field of infinite grace.

HOLE IN THE MOUNTAIN

"It is the celestial ennui of apartments
That brings us back to the first idea."
Wallace Stevens

He wrote about the pink house in the mountains. Plants and trees and flowers grew wild around the house, like a hut in some remote jungle, and the cool air smelled of honeysuckle, apples, and pine trees. On the porch was an empty rocking chair, slightly rocking by itself, creaking, creaking, creaking like a frog. Behind the chair was a window with dark curtains, the wrinkles in the cloth twisting into curves and shadow. The boy in the story — freckle-faced — filled a metal bucket with snow water and walked down the winding driveway away from the pink house. The writer didn't know where the boy was going. The boy had a straw hat and skinny legs the color of mahogany. The more he wrote, the more the writer felt himself transported into the fictional dream, a moment of grace, the moment he lived for. But before he could stop to consider if it were right for the work, he created a dark cloud rising over the mountain. The cloud expanded into the clear sky like black factory smoke, until it took the shape of a tornado — and it violently shot at the pink house. When the eye of the tornado touched down, it bore itself into the earth — dirt flying all over, landing on rose petals, bending wild grass, crushing honeysuckle, blowing the straw hat off the boy's head, water spilling from the sides of the bucket. The writer pulled his fingers away from the keyboard, but it was too late, the language had left a big hole in the mountain.

In speedy free writing, he must have channeled the voice of some disdainful deity, and that was what had caused him to write the hole in the mountain. The writer wanted to delete it right away, but as a rule he didn't edit anything on the first draft, so instead of trying to get rid of the hole and admit a wrong turn in the story, he figured he would write around it.

He'd take out the detail on the second draft.

He wrote on.

But the boy in the story, walking like a puppet with his metal bucket — water slapping against the sides — wasn't even looking where he was going. The boy was aware of the window behind the rocking chair, where the old man watched him, so he didn't see that he was headed right toward the hole. To prevent the boy from falling in, the writer typed things in front of the hole — one thing was "twin baby pine trees" — but the hole swallowed the two trees and spit out the needles.

He wrote a white picket fence in front of the hole, the kind you see in front of the home of a happy family, but that too was sucked in.

The writer grabbed for the tennis ball on his desk and he squeezed. He'd had the ball for years, now flimsy, like the soft belly of a rubber doll, and he had convinced himself that he couldn't write without it.

The words he had written couldn't have fallen into the hole, he reasoned, squeezing the ball, because that would be impossible; rather, the computer recording of the words that gave life to the twin baby pine trees and the white picket fence could not keep up with the speed of his language, his eagerness to write, to watch grow what he hoped would be a good story. He put down the tennis ball, and in front of his computer, he placed the cursor in front of the hole. He retyped "twin baby pine trees," but the image fell into the hole again.

He tried this: "a single pine tree."

Swoosh.

And this: "a clay flower pot."

Swoosh.

He knew then that to keep the hole in the mountain would not only suck away from the mountain's metaphoric and symbolic value (whatever they ended up being), but also that *it*, that is, the hole, would also take on metaphoric and symbolic values of its own. He wanted a happy story set in happy mountains. He had no choice but to get rid of the hole.

Perhaps, he thought, he could save the hole in the mountain for another piece (because the description of the hole, he admitted, was good writing). On the screen he highlighted the text that described the hole, and into his keyboard he entered Control-X, which cut the highlighted text (the hole in the mountain), and then Control-N, which created a new document, and then Control-V which was supposed to paste on the new text.

But nothing appeared on the blank screen.

He hit Control-V a second time, but nothing unloaded, no hole. So he tried taking all the steps again, but nothing appeared on the blank document except for the flashing cursor, and in the upper corner of the screen — under the tool bar — the cartoon dog, the MS Word® Office Assistant, whom the writer had named Droopy. The cartoon dog wagged his tail at the writer, eagerly awaiting the text, as if he would gobble up every word. The writer tried a fourth time, but the hole wouldn't appear on the screen. At last, he said, "Screw it" and returned to the story about the mountain, the boy, and the pink house. He deleted the hole.

The story was going well, that moment of grace that he loved so much, when words came to him and made the hours of his day as light as snowflakes floating in the glow of a porch light.

The boy with the straw hat and overalls was tending to the rams, which he raised for wool. He poured water from a metal bucket into their troughs. He was conscious of his every movement, because he knew that the old man was watching him from out the window of the pink house. Suddenly the boy froze with a horrible sense that something was wrong. He looked around, but slowly, so the old man wouldn't notice.

He put down the metal bucket. He saw that the smallest and cutest of the rams, a ewe actually, the one he called Rainy, was sitting forlornly against the fence. The other rams, braying threateningly to each other, pushed with their jealous horns to get a good suck of the fresh water. Rainy sadly lay in the dirt. He walked toward the ewe to see what was wrong.

But then he felt it.

The old man's eyes were all over him.

He was watching from the window behind the rocking chair, creaking, creaking, creaking, his mouth involuntarily moving as if he were toothlessly chewing oatmeal. He looked at the boy with hate-filled eyes.

"Are you O.K., Rainy?" the boy said to the sad ewe. Then he noticed what he should have noticed before.

One ram was missing.

Ten rams around the water trough plus Rainy made eleven, which meant that one was missing. He looked around. Yes, one was missing. The ram he called Shakespeare, the ram that Rainy was always with, was nowhere in sight. "What's happened to Shakespeare?" he asked Rainy. A thick tear, like wax, slowly fell from Rainy's left eye. The little ewe pointed her nose down the mountain, at a trail between the pine trees. The boy walked down the slope and into the glow of a meadow blooming with golden poppies, the sunlight through the trees reflecting off the flowers, coloring the boy's skin a golden yellow.

Then he slipped. His ankle twisted, and he almost fell into a deep hole in the middle of the meadow.

Where did that hole come from? the boy thought, as he stood up in front of it.

The writer thought this too. He thought he had deleted the hole, but there it was, not only in a different spot, but bigger than before. Before it was barely wide enough for a person to fall into, and the person would have slapped the sides on the way down, but now it was wide enough for a Buick to fall through. The sides of the hole were made of pale smooth rock, and there was no bottom.

The writer couldn't stop it from happening, ten of the old man's rams squealed like demon-possessed pigs and ran down the trail toward the hole and threw themselves into it. Their bodies became tiny dots at the vanishing point of the abyss. The boy put his hands on his head and said, "No, no, please no." The old man would kill him.

Then Rainy ran to the hole and fell in. The boy almost slipped trying to save her, but he grabbed onto the rocky edge and with effort pulled himself up and out of the hole.

The writer had to delete that hole, but the boy in the story wouldn't move away from it because Rainy was his favorite ewe. The boy sat at the edge of the hole, his feet dangling in darkness. The boy had often fantasized about killing the old man, and with the money the old man hid in his bedroom, he would take his Rainy down the mountain and they would travel together. They'd head to California, and he'd get a job. He liked to hug his ewe, because she was as soft as an armful of pillows.

The writer tried to rewrite Rainy into the story, but as soon as she appeared at the edge of the hole — the boy screaming with delight — she fell into the hole again. The boy almost fell in trying to save her. So the writer gave up on the ewe and, just to see what would happen, he wrote in a cat, whose paws tried to grasp onto something as it screamed falling into the abyss, then a dog, who howled and whined on the way down, a goldfish (no noise on the way down), a cow, who mooed, a reindeer, a twitchy nosed hamster, an elephant, the children he never had, three raccoons, and a bucket of mice.

The boy, weighted by depression, began to think about throwing himself into the hole.

The writer couldn't highlight and remove the hole in the mountain without removing the boy, too, unless he hit the delete button for each letter that described the hole, but that would take more time than the boy had. Instead, the writer highlighted the boy, cut him out (Control X) and put him on a new document. The boy looked around at all the blank space. No mountain, no rams, no pink house, only the gray-blue nothingness of the computer screen and a cartoon dog hungrily looking down on him. The boy panicked. He pounded on the screen and yelled to the writer, "Let me out of here!" He looked over his shoulder at the cartoon dog, as if it would attack him.

The writer stood up and walked away from his computer. He paced the floors of his apartment, stepping over winter coats and sweaters, partially-read books, and the black leather case for his laptop. Here was a writing problem he couldn't easily solve.

Back and forth he paced. He grabbed his tennis ball from the desk and squeezed. How? How? He looked out the window. The neighbors across the street, kids, husband and wife, were loading their minivan with luggage. The wife stretched to fasten a pair of skis on the top.

As he much as he tried, he could not get rid of the hole in the mountain, it only grew bigger and eventually it reached the yard, trees and rocks and a metal bucket falling into it.

Meanwhile, on the new document, the boy had nothing to do. He sat in the corner of his gray new world, as far away from Droopy as possible. Droopy eemed to be really hungry, his teeth showing, and he watched the boy's every move.

The boy was relieved when the writer beamed him back to the story.

The story was turning out to be nothing like what the writer wanted to write. After the old man in the pink house found out that all the rams were gone, he beat the boy with a broom handle. He wouldn't let the boy eat, and whenever he passed him in the hallway he threw the boy on the ground and kicked him in the stomach and on the shoulders and on the back.

One day the old man, tired from beating the boy so much, grabbed the keys to his Buick and slammed out the door. He backed out of the driveway. He was going to go to town for a drink, but before he could get down the mountain, his Buick fell into the hole. The boy, overjoyed, began searching his father's room for the hidden money. Scattered about the floors were pornographic magazines, and it smelled of stale semen.

This story sucks, the writer said.

He turned off his computer and went to the kitchen to make lunch. The package of six chicken legs that he had pulled out of the freezer the night before was now defrosted. He ripped the cold plastic, and under the flow of warm water, he caressed each fleshy leg. He lay the six pieces into a glass bowl, and sprinkled them with salt and pepper, and he massaged fresh garlic and basil into the muscles of the legs. Along with frying the legs, he mashed potatoes and boiled corn on the cob. He ate his meal with three glasses of cold water. After lunch, he piled the dirty dishes into the sink and went into his bedroom, pushed the clothes off the mattress onto the floor and lay down, his stomach full. He thought: The boy. What was the point? I should just start something new. Perhaps I could use him in another story because I like his character. Sometimes he's so cute. Freckled face. Cutoffs. Straw hat. Yes, I like that boy, but I want him to be happy.

The writer closed his eyes for a nap, but his eyelids suddenly flashed open.

What if it was too late?

What if the boy, while waiting for the writer, fell into the hole? The writer stood. up, put on his jeans and almost ran to his computer. He opened the flap of the laptop and waited impatiently for it to boot, for the Windows® logo to appear.

But it took so long.

He pictured the boy walking outside near the pink house, and maybe it was night and he couldn't see where he was stepping. The writer grabbed the tennis ball and squeezed. Oh, the boy! But all his impatience didn't make the computer go any faster. He looked up. Out the window he could see that it was cold. The naked tree branches looked cold. The iron-colored air looked cold. Yes, it was cold. Last time he had gone out of his apartment, he had worn his puffy coat, the heavy one with a hood. He felt like a little boy when he walked into the grocery store. A woman, picking vegetables as if for her lover, slowly lifted her gaze and looked across the aisle at him. When he found a cart, he took off the coat and put it in the basket, and it took up more room than his groceries.

Now, at his computer, he pictured the boy slipping, grasping onto the side of the hole, trying to pull himself up. He didn't want to lose that boy, because he knew that something good could come of his character, his life.

He still believed.

At last, the icons appeared on the screen and the writer moved the cursor to the document list. He scrolled through the names of stories and novel starts and letters he had never sent and some he regretfully had sent, a cemetery of titles, "Father of 1,000 Heads" "St Martin in the Fields" "In the Valley of the Whale," but he couldn't find the story about the mountain, the boy and the pink house. What had he called it? Perhaps "The Boy," perhaps, "The Boy, the Mountain and the Pink House," but none of those titles were there, and so he read the list, "Sin Salida" "Return, Return!" "Kathy's Wrist" "Sadness of Days." He saw "This Will Not Last" and "Faces of the Dead" and "I Still Love You," documents he had started but never finished and perhaps would never return to: "Black Meets Black" "On Wenderoth's Disfortune."

He couldn't find the story about the boy and the hole.

No, no, no! Not about the *hole*, it wasn't about the hole but about the mountain. That's when an icy thought grasped him at the back of his neck. As much as he didn't want to believe it, he looked for "Hole in the Mountain" on the document list and he found it. It has really grown, he thought, enough so that it took over the entire document. Although he feared what he would find, he double clicked the document icon. The boy, he expected, would have fallen in.

Suddenly there was a pounding and it continued over and over and he realized it was coming not from the story but from the front door.

Someone came to his home and was knocking at his door.

At first he tried to picture the face of who it could be, but it wouldn't be anyone he knew, maybe a salesperson or Jehovah's Witnesses.

He got up from his desk and answered the door. "Oh, hi."

It was the man from across the street. "Are you all right?" he said.

"Oh, I'm fine," said the writer.

"Well, you're sweating. And you look…Well, anyway, Rainy and I are taking the kids to the mountains for some skiing. I was wondering if you'd be willing to feed our cat again. Just for a couple of days."

"Oh, sure, no problem."

"You sure you're O.K.?"

"Fine, fine. Give my regards to Rainy," he said. He almost said, "She hasn't come over in a while. Doesn't she want to see me anymore?" but he only thought it.

"I sure will," said the neighbor.

"Well, here you go." The neighbor handed the key to the writer, turned around and walked across the snow, across the street, to the minivan where Rainy, hands on her slender hips, tilted her head and frowned at the writer. The family got into the van and drove off. The writer opened his fist and looked at the key in his pink palm.

The boy! he thought.

Back at his desk, the writer gasped at what he saw on the computer screen.

He grabbed his tennis ball and squeezed so hard it almost popped. How could this happen? The hole had grown so big that all the language was gone. The boy was gone and the pink house was gone. Gone was the mountain. Trees crackled and bent and were sucked into the black hole. Stars were sucked into the black hole. The moon, shining full and bright, folded into itself and shot into the black hole. Now the writer was gone.

TWO

PAGE 55

I wandered down the hallways of the old-house-turned bookstore, and for no reason at all, I chose that room over the others, that book over others. I found it in what had probably once been a bedroom. The armchairs were French antiques (Second Empire), and there was a table with a reading lamp. The red velvet drapes were old and faded, and there was a tapestry on one wall, an image of men on horses hunting, following their dogs, chasing some shadowy figure into the trees of a dark forest. The room smelled of old cloth and mothballs, like my grandmother's bedroom in my childhood home. Thousands of books lined the walls, stacked as high as the ceiling. I still tell myself that the fact that I ended up with that book — over the almost endless possibilities — could have been random. What attracted me was the cover, because it was leather-bound, dark red leather, like burnt skin. The lettering, although faded, was gold, cursive script. At first I couldn't make out the words, but I liked the curve of the letters and thought that it was written in a language I didn't understand, maybe Arabic or Hebrew, or maybe some ancient language that wasn't used anymore, like old Egyptian or Babylonian. Maybe I pulled it from the shelf hoping it might have been a forgotten book worth more than the tubercular bookseller realized, maybe some ancient text that might have slipped his attention. Maybe the bookseller thought it was a regular book and put it on the shelf and I could buy it and resell it for a lot of money.

I confess: What most excited me about the bookstore was that the books were so old and plentiful, filling each room of the house. In the main room, where the bookseller suspiciously watched the customers, there was a glass shelf with a lock, behind which were old books worth a lot of money. I was certain that the bookseller — maybe during some wild coughing fit — could have made a mistake and left a valuable volume in this room.

I pulled out the book and held it gently in my hand, and I could feel the imprint years of fingers had made on the smooth, leather cover. I saw now that the book was in English, the title was *The Life Expectancy of the Dog.* The publication date indicated that the book was over eighty years old. I leafed through the pages and randomly read some paragraphs. It was pretty boring prose, dry and clunky, and the subject, dogs, I had no interest in. I was about to put it back on the shelf, but I got this sensation that it was worth more than the bookseller knew. I looked up at the tapestry on the opposite wall, at the black dogs leading the hunters into the forest.

The price written in pencil on the inside cover was cheap, so I kept the book walked down the hallway of the old house, past the other rooms also filled with books. I expected the tubercular bookseller to eye the book and me as if he knew what I was up to, but he just coughed like he was dying, took my paper money into his sticky hand and handed me back my coins. I hardly wanted to touch them, but I shoved them to the bottom of my pocket.

I was in the old part of the city, near the main square, so I decided to sit in an outdoor café and examine my new, old book. I stopped across from the cathedral and ordered a beer. I pulled the book from its bag and leafed through the pages and randomly read sentences and passages. The language was dry, which was enough for me to not want to read on, and I was about to put it back in the sack when a beggar came by the tables. He was dressed in an old sports coat which was far too big for him and oversized shoes he must have pulled from the garbage. He went from table to table with his hand out, so I pretended to be reading the book when he approached me.

"Please help me get some food," he said.

I pretended to be so absorbed in the book that I didn't notice him. He stood there for a long time — I could see his shadow slide across the yellowing pages of the book — but I pretended the reading was too good to put down. I turned the next page and read. It was quite boring, something about predicting the future behavior of a dog by identifying the species.

"I'm very hungry. Please," the beggar said.

I thought of the coins with the bookseller's phlegm sticking to the bottom of my pockets, but I didn't much feel like touching them, so I continued to pretend to read.

That was when it occurred to me that this book was worth nothing. I felt foolish for wasting money on it, but I would waste no more. I saw the shadow of the beggar's hand perfectly projected on a page of the book, his fingers trembling. I pretended to be so into reading that I didn't notice him. Finally he seemed to be leaving, his hand sliding away, but now, as I recall it, I'm certain he said something like "May you die reading that book."

I pretended not to hear him. I continued to read (or pretended to read) until the shadow of the beggar's body moved away. I looked up, and suddenly the trumpets from the cathedral sounded the new hour. I looked down at the page number I had been reading and saw that it was page seven. I got this feeling, this strong feeling of doom. An idea suddenly occurred to me: If I didn't read to at least the page number of my age, 55, then I would die. I don't know why I felt this, but it was such a strong feeling that I thought it must have come from some place other than me. It was such boring prose, but I read on, and what could have been hours later, I finally reached page 55. Relieved, freed from the beggar's curse, I looked up from the book and saw him across the plaza, hand out for money, walking around the tables in his oversized shoes. I remembered the shadow of his hand on the pages, and for some reason — some stupid reason — I was struck by the idea that the curse was worse than I had thought at first. I believed that as many pages of the book that I read was how long my life would be. If I only read to page 55, I would die at age 55. Now, I try to remember why this occurred to me, but for some reason, I pictured the photos hanging on the walls around my grandmother's house, all those sepia-colored faces of family who died before I was even born, looking down on me, as if expecting something from my life that might justify theirs. I kept reading. I stopped for awhile at page 66, but I didn't want to die at 66. That wasn't enough. Eleven more years wasn't enough.

I went back to reading, reading all day long until the shadows of the cathedral grew so long and wide that they covered the plaza with darkness — including the white pages of my book. The lamps around the square flickered on, and I could hear music starting from the bars and nightclubs. I imagined young people dancing in a frenzy of sweat and light. I was only on page 72. I kept reading, even after the first waiter left and another took over my table. I ordered another beer, though I hadn't touched the first one. I read and read, and when I got to page 122, I figured that was enough. My life would be long enough if I were to die at 122.

I would have stopped there, but some idea struck me: I hadn't understood a word of what I had read.

I knew nothing more about the life of a dog than I had before. I couldn't recall a single fact from the book, couldn't quote a single passage. What if I lived to be an old man, 122, but what if I went through life the way I went through the pages of that book, that is, without understanding? I would be an invalid with no thought, no sense, no one to care for me. My sister, already 60 years old, would be dead by then, so who would be left? What a miserable way to live, unable to understand anything around you, unable to enjoy even your own thoughts, because you have no thoughts.

What if the way we read a book is the way we live our lives? If we can't stand the reading and are always looking toward the bottom of the page, toward the end of the chapter, counting how many pages until the end of the book, surely we must live life the same way, impatient with a walk in the city or with sitting in a garden, wanting only to arrive, never to be. What a waste that would be, to run through the pages of my life like an idiot. I made the decision to go back to page seven, where the text started, and to reread, this time to understand as many pages as I could, the way I wanted to live life.

It was almost impossible to get through a few pages, because every page number, starting with number seven, made me remember something from that age in my life. Memories attacked me. On page seven, I remembered when I was seven, out in the yard raking leaves. I looked up and saw into the window of my grandmother's room. She stood before a mirror looking at herself, yelling at herself with hatred. I tried to ignore it, to rake harder, to hear the thousand leaves piling up, but her sharp voice kept reaching my ears.

Each page number would flood me with more memories, some I hadn't recalled in years, memories I didn't want to recall. It must have taken me several hours just to get to my teen years, after my grandmother's suicide, when my sister was left to take care of me. I could barely stand page 22, because that was a bad time in my life, but I read on, trying to understand the text and forget the memories. I would read an entire page, but I when reached the bottom, I realized I hadn't understood anything. I kept reading and re-reading. I'm still reading. I'm on page 55 now. I seem to be stuck on this page, because I understand nothing about page 55. I think I do, but then I'm about to change the page, to go to 56, but then I realize I don't know what I have just read. I don't want to live like that. What would be the point of a long life if you can't understand it? So I keep returning back to that page, number 55. I'm reading even now — or trying to — but things get in the way. I've forgotten how old I am.

CALABI YAU

Call it a vision/don't call it a vision, but before the man even moved into the big, white house by the river, he knew he would meet her. When he passed by the house for the first time, it came to him, an image, a vision of her standing in the back door of that house, looking out at the path to the water, calling for someone, maybe him. Her long red hair was why he knew he was having a vision into the future, because he knew no one who looked like her. He knew too that when he would see her for the first time in real life, he would recognize her.

A vision like this wasn't normal for the man, and he normally wouldn't have believed it. He was rational, and if anything could be said about his compositions, his symphonies and scores, it would be just that: they were logical. Beautiful at times, yes, he had to admit, when the form of the piece called for such convention, but logical, measured and precise. He rarely allowed the notes to fly away from his control like spirits, because his music was an expression of an idea, an argument for a metaphysical or scientific stance, and that was what made him successful. That was what kept him working.

He looked at several more houses, some much more efficient and newer than the house by the river, but every time he pictured the old white house, he remembered the girl with the red hair. She's looking out the back door, calling for someone, and somehow he knew — even though he would never usually give in to such superstition — that if he moved into that house, he would meet her. He imagined that she would become (whoever she was/is/could be) someone intimate with him.

At 35 years old, he had already done the Hollywood thing, because when he was 25, he was commissioned by a college friend-turned-producer to do a soundtrack for a movie that became a blockbuster. It thrust him into money and reputation. He was nominated for an Oscar®. He had ten years of being young and successful in L.A., ten years of writing music on the veranda of his beach house and partying at night. He wrote the score for a popular horror flick, hack work but profitable, and although he was from Fresno, now his friends were industry people on both coasts. He went to a lot of parties, but when he reached thirty-five years old, something happened.

Not an epiphany, not a sublime moment watching birds in the field, and not an anagogical vision of a tree blowing angry in the wind, he just woke up and knew the truth of it. It was time to move on to more serious music. He had the means to write full-time for the rest of his life, if he lived modestly. He wanted to get out of the L.A. area and live in some isolated place to just write.

What he wanted to write obsessed him, the musical notes following him into his dreams, and he took this to mean that it needed to be written.

It was a symphony. The energy of it had been pulsing within him for years, trying to seep out of his every pore. At any random time he might see the musical notes written in the air, or he'd hear the sounds coming to him. The fact was, this music, this symphony, this idea had been with him ever since he was five years old. The rhythm used to come to him in a recurring nightmare. It started each night with a one-two beat of the same note, B flat, on an instrument that sounded like a cello. Over and over it went on, one-two, one-two, the same note, no variation, tense in its monotone, and that sound would take him into a dream that he hated but kept coming back to. He was five years old. He was in a car at night. He was alone. He was on the floor in the backseat. He was scrunched up, hiding from something bad. That one-two beat of the same cello — *da da, da da* — became the sound of crickets. Whoever was outside of the car wanted to kill him.

Now he knew that the one-two beat would be in his new symphony, but he didn't want it to be about that, not *that* feeling or *that* memory. He wanted it to be metaphysical, not emotional. It would be about the extra six dimensions predicted by quantum mechanical String Theory. He knew it would get recorded and that it would sell well, because suddenly everyone was into the new physics. It would be a string theory ensemble, cello, viola, violin, guitar, lute, and harp, six instruments, a musical journey into each of the six dimensions predicted by the mathematics of physics, each instrument acting as a guide, a Virgil if you will, through the other dimensions. The symphony would culminate with all the instruments sounding at once, dissonant and fragmented, a cacophony of quantum chaos, which would represent reality at the subatomic level, inside the atoms and the nuclei and the quarks.

These extra dimensions were curled up and twisted — not like a child in the backseat of a car — but curled up on the sub-atomic level. He wanted each movement to represent leading into and out of those dimensions, but logically, un-emotionally, and that one-two beat of the cello would go on for about five minutes, that single note over and over again, until it became like the measured sound of logic, until there was nothing left to feel.

He decided he would buy the white house by the river. The first week was just getting all of his stuff from the beach house in L.A. After he moved in, he took a week or so arranging his things, his books on the shelves, the way he wanted to place his antique musical instruments on the walls, his framed awards and certificates, his Oscar® shining atop a bookshelf. The main room was very large, containing both the living room and the formal dining room, and during the day he kept the curtains open. He liked glowing in so much sunlight, and he left all the windows open so he could feel the breeze and hear the river. It wasn't until he started working on his symphony that he met the girl with the red hair.

She rang his doorbell. He was a bit impatient, because he was getting some good writing done and he didn't want the interruption, but he got up anyway and answered it. She stood in the frame, holding a baking pan wrapped with foil.

"Hot beans," she said. She smiled and stood there, as if she expected him to let her in, or maybe she wanted him to comment on how good the food smelled, or maybe she wasn't thinking anything at all, just feeling the muscles in her forearms starting to hurt from holding the pan. "Hot beans," she said. She wanted him to take the pan.

"Uh, thanks," he said, taking the pan.

She wore a red summer skirt and a white sleeveless blouse, and her hair was loose, glowing with sunlight. "You have very beautiful hair," he said.

She touched it. "Thanks," she said. "Am I late?"

"I'm sorry, come in," and he stepped out of the way.

She walked into the house as if she were walking into a place she had always wanted to see. She looked up at the instruments on the high part of the wall, old violins, string instruments from Elizabethan times, and flutes and harmonicas and clarinets.

"Wow," she said. "Some collection."

"I'm a musician," he said.

"Oh, *are* you?" she asked, looking him up and down, as if she had ideas about musicians.

He held the beans, feeling himself under her scrutiny, his forearms getting tired. He could smell them, and they smelled good, a rich tomato-based sauce with garlic.

"Where is everybody?" she asked. "Out back by the river?

"Everybody?"

"You're not Rick?"

That was when it occurred to them both. She was at the wrong house. Her friends were having a potluck at another friend's place by the river, a friend she hadn't yet met. "How embarrassing," she said.

"I thought you were the welcome wagon," he said.

"Well, welcome," she said.

"I guess you'll want your beans back."

She laughed and asked if he wanted to try a bowl. They were really good, she said. He said he'd love some, and he brought out two clay bowls and he served some for both of them. The soup was thick. He opened a bottle of wine. By the second glass, she admitted to him that she was kind of glad she had gotten the wrong house, because it would be better to show up late. Maybe, she said, on a subconscious level she had done it on purpose, who knows the realities we create for ourselves, she said. Her friends wanted to fix her up with that Rick guy, and she had no desire to be fixed up.

"So you're single?" he asked, perking up.

"Well, yeah," she said, as if the answer were obvious. He said his name was Brad. She said her name was Alyssa.

She never ended up going to that potluck or meeting Rick. A month later she was practically living with Brad in the white house by the river.

The relationship was ideal. She worked in the daytime, so he could work all day on his symphony while she was gone, and in the late afternoon when he couldn't work anymore, she was just getting home. They would spend the evenings walking along the river or cooking elaborate meals. She loved to cook and was a genius in the kitchen. He loved good wines, and they opened a bottle each night, tasting it, commenting on it, writing notes in their wine journal. Sometimes she would come home for lunch. He stepped out of his study, where he wrote, and she would be sitting at the table eating a salad.

"I brought a sandwich for you," she'd say.

It was the best relationship he had ever been in, and he found himself wanting to marry her, wanting her to move in all her stuff. She was a teacher, so she would have summers off, and they could travel all over the world, anywhere in the world.

Things were so perfect, so wonderful, until one day they got in a big fight. He forgot what had started it, but it was bad. They yelled and screamed and cried, and he said some things to her that were so mean, so vicious, that she said she was leaving and never coming back. She took all her stuff, threw it into her car and drove off with squealing tires.

For the next few days he got no writing done, nor did he sleep. One day, after many days of drinking wine and not sleeping, he was in his study writing, or trying to write, and he began to fade out. He closed his eyes and entered that first stage of sleep, where things began to lose their form, and the Lady of the Lake was taking him on a boat, across the water to the dream world. He could hear her wooden paddle swish and pop in the water. Suddenly the truth slapped him awake.

Alyssa never existed. Brad realized that he had made her up, based on the vision he had had the first day he had driven by the house. That would explain why they never went into town for dinner. Everyone else would see a man alone, sitting across empty space, talking to empty space, leaning over the tabletop and kissing empty space. That was why he had never met any of her friends, and the one time a friend of his came to visit him from Hollywood, she wasn't around.

But of course, this idea was ridiculous, he told himself. Of course she existed. They had gotten into a fight. That was all.

One night he walked around the house to look for anything she might have left behind, a sock, some underwear, a book she was reading, but he found nothing, no sign of her. This either meant that she didn't exist or that she was so angry at him that she had taken everything of hers, and that wasn't a good sign. It meant she was serious about never coming back.

He drank more, forgot to sleep. Sometimes, he hallucinated, thinking he saw her walking across the floors of the main room or standing at a window looking out or walking to the river in the moonlight in a see-through nightgown.

Maybe he was too absorbed in his work to think correctly, maybe he was going nuts, but maybe, just maybe there was no such girl as Alyssa. If you think about it, the name itself, Alyssa, sounded like a male fantasy. Of course she would be called Alyssa. Why couldn't her name be Bertha or Martha?

One night he paced around the house, walking barefooted through the rooms, wondering where was reality. He reached a door at the end of the hallway, the door to his bedroom. It was closed. If he were to allow it, could he enter that door to a room he had never seen? Maybe he could walk into the downtown of some big city, from his dimly-lit hallway to a canyon of tall office buildings. He opened it, but it was just his empty bedroom. On the nightstand, next to his bed, was a box of Kleenex.

One night, he went back to his symphony, and he wrote an entire dimension in one sitting, expressed through the guitar, and it had an actual melody, the music of love. As he heard the music in his head and wrote it down, he imagined fingers coming out of the river, thousands of fingers twittering in the moonlit water.

That was the night he went out there. It was dark. He walked out the back door, walked through bushes and ancient trees, walked to the sound of the water. On the bank, he heard the river's great rush, as if darkness made it louder. It was the loudest symphony, ever. The last thing he saw as he slipped and fell into the cold fingers of the water was himself as a little boy, hiding in the backseat of a car, on the floor, curled up and twisted.

The next morning, Alyssa woke up believing she could forgive him for what he had said. She drove to his house. She knocked at the door, but there was no answer, so she was going to enter with her key, but she didn't have it. She didn't remember taking it off her keychain, but it wasn't there. She tried the door, and it was unlocked. She entered the cold house. The place seemed too quiet. She called for him, went from room to empty room.

She went into the kitchen and saw the back door. She opened it, stood in the frame, feeling the fresh morning air. She heard the sound of the river. She called out to him. "Brad," she said, surprised to hear the panic in her voice. "Brad, honey, are you there?"

THE GIFT

The untitled canvas was promised to me, or to be fair, to *us*, by Alfredo Galindo Machado. I received it over two years after his now infamous death. Men in white pulled up in a white van to our building and unloaded the wooden crate. It was as large as a gorilla cage, as if Galindo Machado himself was inside of it ready to jump out. The three delivery boys carried the box up the winding stairs to my apartment, and they set it on the wooden floors — the reflection on the shiny parquets stretching the box and me and the delivery boys in their white overalls. I offered them a glass of water. They declined and asked me to sign the delivery slip. They left, one after another. I heard their feet on the winding stairs, saw their shadows on the walls descend into the street.

I knew that no one had seen this painting, because Galindo Machado had promised us that he would keep it secret, that it was only for Jonathan and me, a gift. Rumors of the unseen canvas spread after I received the crate, "a painting by the man whose work caused riots." I got calls from reporters and collectors and friends asking to see the painting, but I denied it existed, not for selfish reasons, but from some uncertainty whether or not it was right to make public what was meant to be private.

Even weeks after the delivery boys had left the crate on the floor, I was too afraid to open it. What if what was inside was too intimate? What would it be like to show a painting so innovative that it could only be misunderstood by most? And even if it were celebrated as "great", access to the work could take away its power, render it kitschy, like Bach's Toccata and Fugue in D Minor for pipe organ, played over and over, ad naseum to indicate kitschy-spooky haunted houses.

Dum! Dum! Du Duuum!

That once lovely work of organ became images of Halloween, Count Chocula breakfast cereal, and Elvira, Mistress of the Dark.

Dum! Dum! Du Duuuuum!

I wouldn't allow Galindo Machado's work to be drained of its power by a too-eager audience. I would keep it a secret.

One art collector called me and told me that if the painting really existed, it was an historical event for all art, and he'd pay me whatever price I wanted for it, sight unseen. "I inherited some land," he said. I hung up on him, but he called back and begged me to allow him to just see it, just one glimpse at whatever price.

"There is no such painting," I said firmly into the phone and hung up again.

More and more time passed. María, who cleaned my apartment, tried to move it aside so she could sweep and polish the floors underneath it, but it was too heavy. She swept around it, and a few weeks later, she placed a Tiffany lamp and a vase with a yellow flower on top of it. It became a piece of furniture.

Several times a day I passed by the crate. As I walked from room to room, I couldn't help but feel its presence, like the cage of the "Hunger Artist" in the middle of the town square. Inside of that box I imagined an emaciated man, shriveled and withered from hunger and thirst.

In dim afternoon light when the drapes were drawn, the crate seemed to contain the color red, which gave a pinkish tone to the wood which held it, as if it were pulsing like a human organ. Several times I grabbed my claw hammer from the tool drawer, but something didn't feel right about seeing it without Jonathan, even though he was gone for good, that is, even though he was dead.

Galindo Machado had meant it for both us. "Ningun ojos antes de ustedes," he had said, until you two (Jonathan and I) see it.

We had been in a gallery at a showing when he first told us about the painting. He had pulled us aside, away from the food table and white napkins and stem glasses and green conversations. He looked nervous, as if he were about to confess a murder.

"I painted something for you two," Galindo Machado told us. "I can't describe it."

Jonathan, always taking control, tried to tutor him into expressing it. "What is the most striking thing about it? The color? The texture?"

"No, no," he said, his eyes so full of fear you might think that he was about to confess a murder. "The most striking thing about the painting is. . .the *dead.*"

He sounded so corny I could almost hear the first kitschy notes of Toccata and Fugue in D Minor.

Dum! Dum! Du Duuuum!

I laughed.

Jonathan looked at me admonishingly. Then he looked softly at Galindo Machado, by now an old man, bald, pointy ears, a nervous twitch in his upper lip, a Picasso archetype.

"Death's one of the oldest sources of artistic inspiration, no?" Jonathan asked the old man.

"You don't understand. The *subject* is not death." He looked around, making sure no one was listening, and then he leaned in close and was about to say something else. His breath smelled of garlic and wine. Suddenly he was pulled away from us by his agent to meet some people. Jonathan looked at me. "I think the old man has lost it. Nothing new about painting and the dead and the dying and all that duende stuff that gets old real fast. Still, it's got to be a powerful image," he said. He raised his champagne glass, the sparkling bubbles rising up the surface like tiny souls.

As much as anyone, Jonathan was responsible for the fame of Galindo Machado. In his first book on hyperrealism, he devoted an entire chapter to the unknown Chicano artist, a cholo from the barrio who would rise to such greatness and fame during his lifetime that you only had to mention two of his names, Galindo Machado, to conjure his images. His most controversial painting was called the *Bloody Mary*. It so offended the Chicano/a and Catholic communities that he received death threats. He became a symbol of all that was hated in the Chicano community, sell-outism, art so expensive only the rich could afford it, irreverence of La Cultura.

I was a Chicano, too, a former activist in college, where I had been president of MEChA. I had organized walkouts and strikes. By the time I met Jonathan, my revolutionary fervor had become my insistence on buying whole organic coffee beans from a co-op, and grinding them myself each morning. I became a Culture and Entertainment reporter for *The LA Times*.

Galindo Machado refused to speak about what he intended with the *Bloody Mary*, because he said, he wanted the painting to speak for itself. At one opening in Fresno, CA, the painting caused a riot. Chicano activists threw rocks in the gallery rooms that had his work, and they yelled curses at him and his partner Marta as they stepped out of their car.

Jonathan then wrote an entire book about Galindo Machado, comparing his work, the reaction of it, to Stravinsky. He argued that there was something in the Chicano's work that indicated there would be not only a shift in Chicano art, but also in the art world as a whole, a radical new vision.

He wrote that Galindo Machado's works showed that the artist sought to shatter the very weakness of his early paintings, the reality of hyperrealism. For many years he had painted photograph-accurate images, and it took a trained eye to tell the difference between one of his oils and a blown-up photograph. Some people suggested that he must have enlarged photos, that he couldn't have painted with such accuracy, but he was that good.

Once, I had seen him painting what turned out to be *Bloody Mary*. I had dropped by unexpectedly at his studio in Santa Monica, saw him standing before the giant canvas, red and blue streaks of paint trailing from his brush. His stereo was playing some sort of New Age music, a cello moaning a repetitive beat. It was not so much a conventional melody as a triangle of tones, one-two-three beats, the same three notes over and over again, redundant, maybe a b flat. The tone only slightly changed its pitch after three notes of the triangle.

Do do do
do do do
do do do

Do do do
do do do
do do do

Over and over again.

I sat on a stool and watched as Galindo Machado slapped the canvas with quick brush stokes, *do do do* **do** *do do*. He was not even aware that I was there. Sunlight blasted into the studio.

Shortly after Jonathan's first book, four of us were having dinner. Galindo Machado was accompanied by Marta, an Argentine woman with short black hair and a thin face with sunken cheeks. She wore light blue sweaters and smoked a lot. She always carried a bottle of water. There was something edgy about her beauty, not like she was dangerous, but something sharp and structured, like the thin angle of her bones, her elbows, her shoulders in a tanktop.

The artist, at that time only in his forties, was a rising star. He pulled out his sketch pad. He drew us sitting around the table drinking wine, eating.

Years later, Marta would leave him for a Dutch painter popular in Europe, who specialized in painting bricks and human feces. After that, Galindo Machado painted with a frenzy for twenty years, remarrying a few times. Then he killed himself. They found his body almost drained of its blood. Red smudges, like a child's drawings, were all over the walls of his bedroom. His mattress and sheets were soaked with blood. In his hand he held a suicide note, but the blood washed away many of the characters. I wouldn't find out about the note until later, a year after Galindo Machado died. A year after that, Jonathan died. I suppose I'm next.

Galindo Machado's suicide note said that the crate (at such and such studio) should be sent to our address, in Venice Beach, so two years after his death, the delivery boys brought it over.

It was hard to sleep at night with that unopened box in the other room.

At night, when all the lights were out, red light from within the crate spilled onto the living room floor. It seemed to spread like oozing liquid down the hallway to my bedroom door at the end, through the crack at the bottom. The light crawled up my bed, spread over my comforter, and it rested on the whiteness of my pillowcase.

One night I called some friends and we met at a bar and got drunk. I stayed out very late, and perhaps I was getting drunk so I could lose my fear. As I walked home, I pretended that Jonathan was walking with me. I told him that I was going to open it.

I entered my apartment, and I stood before the unopened crate. I saw a blur of shadow coming from the kitchen. I turned and saw the doorway. I put the Tiffany lamp on the floor, and the vase with the flower, and I grabbed my claw hammer. I began to pry open the top, pulling out the nails and prying more, sweating and heaving with the effort. I could smell the wood. I could taste the sour alcohol on my breath.

I unlidded the crate.

The painting was wrapped several times over in newspaper. I ripped out the paper and let it fly all over the floor, a laugh sneaking out of me. There was so much newspaper, so many headlines in English and Spanish, floating all over the room, the crumpled images of smiling presidents, buildings crumbled by wartime, colored advertisements for new dresses and hats and cars and washing machines. All those shreds floated to the ground. Then I reached the final wrappings around the canvas. Black sheets. I peeled off a sheet only to reveal another. I threw the first on the floor and then another.

The blinds in the window were turning orange with morning sun. The black sheets I had thrown around the box looked like a circle of Arab women on their knees, bent over in prayer.

I unwrapped the last black sheet.

It.

How can I describe it?

If it took such a master all his life to create it, how I could I, a minor journalist, recreate it with words? The dominant color was red, the brush strokes thick and disturbed, like Van Gogh's skies. Swirls of dried paint formed a red circle on black. But the sadness.

How can I describe such sadness? Abstract language couldn't describe it, it was so powerful that no string of words could join in the air and evoke the sadness. It was an imageless image, more energy than form, more perfect than music. To describe it with language I would have to rely on the cheap tricks of poetry, similes and metaphors, verbal expressions that would attempt to get across the idea, which meant it had to be converted into an idea.

Could I say that it was sad as dead children in a mass grave?

That doesn't even come close. I am impotent.

Sadder than an armless lady begging at the church doors?

Nothing works. Nothing. Sad like an empty chair in the yellow weeds? Like a child's ball on the floor of an empty room? Like a woman walking across a bridge at night in the rain? No *thing*. Like the way you sounded when you moaned in your bed as a child? A cello groaning in an empty room? Jonathan's shriveled face in the open coffin? A skateboard belly-up in the sand? Rose petals spilling from the hands of a child? A lone tree on a foggy hill? A train at night in the rain in an abandoned rail yard? A used suitcase rolling off a garbage heap? A pair of gnarled work boots on a cement porch? The moon bleeding in the mouth of a woman?

The next day I avoided looking at the painting. María came to clean. As always when she comes to my home, I left her in peace and walked along the boardwalk at Venice. A few hours later, I was walking in the garden behind our building, every now and then sitting on a stone bench, reading from a now-forgotten book I had brought with me. I heard footsteps on the path. The cleaning lady came out of the bushes. She told me she was finished.

I took out my wallet and counted the bills, and for some reason, I included an extra twenty dollars. I closed the palm of her hand. "Thank you," I said.

She looked up at me, almost admiringly, and she said, "That's a fine painting you have, sir. So beautiful."

"Which painting?" I asked.

"The new one."

"You like it?" I asked, surprised that she would respond to such an abstract piece.

"So beautiful," she said, her face aglow. "Such tenderness."

She slowly opened her bag, and pulled out a worn wallet, the fake leather peeling away from the cloth. She snapped it open, unzipped a compartment, folded the bills into a tiny square, and placed them inside. Then she zipped, snapped, put the wallet back into the bag. She looked at me. "So beautiful," she said. "But I'm more than a little surprised that you would have a painting of the Lord Jesus Christ."

"The *wha?*"

She looked at me gently. "Good day, sir," she said. And she left me alone in the garden.

SOUL LIBRARY

"Etiam oblivisci quod scis interdum expedit!"

'd call it a journey, but that hardly gives you an idea of what that place was like. I never want to see it again, yet I feel as if I'm still there, or occasionally I fall back into it, like falling into a dream. I never want to go back, ever, and I hope I have forgotten enough of it to keep me sane.

How can I explain this place?

Some mystics, including Swedenborg, Cayce, *et al* believe that everything we do, everything we see or think, every one of our acts are recorded in our souls. Even if we don't remember most of these "soul entries," they still make up who we are in the spiritual world. When we die, the mystics say, we are not the body, we are not the exterior person; rather, our memories make up our interior person, and that will give shape to our spiritual bodies.

If this is true, then there is a great gap between our earthly memory and our soul memory, which being accessible after death seemed like such a waste, since we couldn't use it while we were still alive.

What if we remembered every image we had seen or every passage in a book we had read or every scene from every movie we had ever watched?

Like all humans, I forgot more than I retained, and that bothered me. It bothered me when I picked up a book to read and half way through realized I had already read it, it bothered me when I rented a movie and watched it most of the way through before an image within it reminded me that I had already seen it. Why couldn't I remember all that information? What a waste of time, I thought, to read if I'm going to forget what I read. Plato said "To learn is to remember." I became obsessed with devising a way to access those memories.

I started recording my thoughts on tape, that is, my thoughts on what I was reading, so I wouldn't forget what I had read. As I played back the tape, I heard myself commenting about a particular passage I had found important. For example, in *The World as Will,* Schopenhauer tells us that music corresponds to desire, and that the low notes from a cello correspond to a low level of desire, a sort of desire of the aged, infused with wisdom. I recalled Blochs's *Schelomo,* wherein the cello represents the voice of Solomon. I was struck by the passage as I read it, so I spoke it into the tape recorder.

About a week later I had already made so many tapes based on my reading that I had to stay up late at night reviewing them, and I was shocked how much information I had forgotten in such a short time. As I listened to my recordings of Schopenhauer, I was blown away a second time not only by the idea of the cello and desire, but by the fact that I had forgotten about it. If this happened with the few recordings I had made, then it came to reason that there were many important passages I had read and forgotten about.

My other memory, my soul memory, according to Cayce et al., didn't forget that passage by Schopenhauer, just my earthly memory, the one contained in my brain. Very little of my memory belonged to me, the person, the man (to quote Whitman) "between my hat and shoes." If I only had access to the soul memory. I could go through the shelves of my mind and pull things out. How many great thoughts from Great books and how many varied things did I have recorded in my memory but couldn't access? How my research suffered, and now, I was an old man, and although I had written many books, none of them were going to give me immortality. Most of my books were out of print. I was close to dying, but first I wanted to write my *magnum opus*. I would have sold my soul to the devil (if I had believed in the devil) if the devil would allow me access to my Soul Library.

It would make me the most learned scholar in the universe. Even if what one has read has been limited, this would be true. If we retained the memory of everything observed, all images, all newspaper articles and magazines, all we have seen on TV and in the movies, we would have a great wealth of information.

I was a full professor of Philosophy and Religion at the University of Minnesota, but I was originally from California and my family was from Mexico. I had never been married, never knew how to talk with women, and on winter vacations I went to see my family. One Christmas (and herein begins the unbelievable journey) we as a family decided we would meet at my great aunt's house in Tepotztlán, México, the matriarch of our clan. She was very near to the age of dying. It was a small town surrounded by jagged mountains, a place that has been sacred for many generations to the indigenous people. A lot of North Americans who practiced witchcraft and sorcery, believing the land to contain some sort of spiritual energy, had moved there and opened up crystal shops and sold items of the occult, tarot cards, etc. I never believed in such things, and the locals tolerated them for the revenue they brought into the town, but they never took them too seriously.

One night after dinner I was taking a walk alone through the cobblestone streets.

I walked across the dark plaza, where some stray dogs were hanging out sniffing each other, and to the old cathedral, built in the time of Cortez, and crumbling now, sinking in to the earth, a little lopsided. I saw that there was an old man on the steps. He was selling books on the Aztec language. I guess it should have struck me as strange that he would be there that late at night, when no one was around but shadows and the distant howls of dogs and coyotes. For some reason I stopped and smoked a cigarette with him. I see now that this man must have been some sort of demon, or at any rate, a spirit not from this world, but at the time I didn't believe such things. Nevertheless, there was something weird about him. The cigarette tip lit up his face when he took a drag from it, a face half as old as time.

Inside of his eyes were pins of blue light. I stamped out my cigarette, gave him an extra for later, and I was about to walk back to my great aunt's house when he said, "I know how to get you there."

"What are you talking about?" I asked him.

"The place where memory is kept," he said.

I was shocked, and in retrospect, I wondered if I had told him about my desire and forgot about it (but of course, that can't be true. What can be forgotten now?)

The old man held out his open palm, and inside he had a tiny pellet. "Take this," he said. "But make sure that this is what you really want."

I took the pellet just to get rid of the crazy man, and I held it in my shirt pocket for several days, not thinking much about it but always feeling it throbbing next to my heart. I was ignorant, and I figured what the old man had given me was a pellet of peyote. One night, I decided I would eat it, because if anything, I would understand more the works of Antonin Artuad, who came to Mexico to experiment with peyote, and the writings of Carlos Casteneda, whom I always considered a shallow scholar and a poor prose writer, although I had read seven volumes of his work.

One night, when the cries of the coyote were coming from the mountains and white moths flew in and out of the bedroom window, I took the pellet, just to see what would happen. After two hours, I felt nothing, no effect, and I dismissed the old man as crazy.

But then I feel asleep. I dreamed I was walking into a library. It was huge, the walls made of part stone, part brick, and part wood, as if the builders had run out of material and had just used whatever they had left. Still, the library was huge and gray and reached high up into the heavens. I could see the stars. I walked into a giant entrance, into a foyer, walls as tall as a canyon. Hanging way up high on the walls were paintings of the faces of people I had known but who had died. These portraits were far up on the walls, but each one had a ladder, leaning against the wall, that led to the face. There were ladders everywhere, as I was old, and I knew a lot of dead.

I walked into an arched doorway, on the other side of which were hallways leading to an infinite amount of rooms, and it occurred to me that even though I was dreaming, I was standing at the entrance of my soul library.

I was elated. I arbitrarily chose a hallway and went down it. I saw that all the rooms had doors made of different material, some of wood, some of corrugated tin. I would learn that the interior of each room was round, like our brains, round like time itself. Even the roofs and floors in the rooms were round. Most of the rooms had piles of books I had read, and at the moment I walked in, I remembered every detail from every book in that room. Information and voices and images flooded my memory and filled my brain up so much that I felt like I would collapse from the weight. I remembered insignificant information like names and dates, and I remembered characters and details from every novel in that room. I remembered wardrobe closets and weapons of battle. I went crazy with glee at such memory. I felt smarter with that first room, eager to explore more. I ran out of one room into the hallway and into another room, all of them like the others, all lined with books I had read and forgotten, all of the information infusing my memory so that I could recite passages for every thought that occurred to me. Just think how I could impress my colleagues, I thought, and show them how superior I am to them. I could recall so many passages, word for word, and the contents within which those passages were written, and even the page numbers on which they appeared, and the publisher and the edition.

I remembered mathematical equations and maps, graphs and tables, but that wasn't all. I remembered the placement of every comma on every page I had read. I remembered semicolons and colons and parenthetical comments and all the footnotes I had ever seen. I ran from room to room gleeful to recall how many good books I had read. Then something strange happened.

I realized that I was remembering something else, something like a shadow spreading across memory's light. I not only remembered the contents of the books, but I could also recall where I was when I was reading them and what my thoughts were at the time — but not only that.

I remembered and felt the emotions I was feeling at the time I was reading. This is impossible to explain with language, but I felt all these things at the same time that I re-re-received the knowledge, emotions I hadn't felt in years, emotions I forgot I had ever had.

It was overwhelming. I had to stop in the hallway for rest. At first there was silence in those hallways.

I heard my own breathing.

Then suddenly my head was flooded with sound, all the sounds I had ever heard in my lifetime, at an intense volume, a din. I ran down the hallway, trying to get rid of everything in my head. I reached what I thought was the exit from the library, but it was an entrance into another room filled with more books, ones from my youth. I recalled the face of Nora, the girl I had loved more than anyone, ever, and I wanted to forget. I had forgotten her — how had I forgotten? — but now I remembered I was reading a book as I ate my lunch in the employees' break room, and she was on the other side the glass, on the main floor of the office. I was 19 years old. It was an insurance office. I had forgotten how I never talked to her at the office. I wanted to, but I never got the nerve. I worked there as an undergrad, and I just watched her, I was a shy boy, I just watched her carrying files across the floor, laughing, looking at the picture frames she had of her parents on her desk. I recalled every detail of her face, her hands, the material of her skirts and blouses, and the way, before leaving the office, she put on her coat, untied her red hair. I remembered the time she smiled at me.

I ran out of that room, looking for the exit, and I entered into one that didn't have books, but video monitors on which played TV shows, movies, documentaries, all video imagery and sound-links I had seen and heard in my lifetime, including the most forgotten episodes (in their entirety) of "The Simpsons," "Bewitched," and "The Land that Time Forgot." There were TV shows I had completely forgotten about, plays, movies, puppet shows, and now I could recall every detail, every line of dialogue, and what I was feeling at the time.

I used to watch TV when depression overcame me, the loneliest times of my stupid life. Sadness came back to me now, like a flood of despair. I ran out of the room, down the hallway, down many hallways, looking for the exit, wanting out. I came to a room with a leather armchair and newspapers and magazines, casual reading and the emotions and memories of the time I was reading them. In another room there was a kitchen table, yellow, Formica-topped, and all over the surface of the table and on the shelves of cupboards were cereal boxes and newspaper-comic sections, horoscopes, crossword puzzles, all those thing that over a lifetime I occupied myself with as I ate alone. I remembered the moans of my mother dying of cancer as I ate a bowl of Lucky Charms.

Finally, I ran into a black, empty room.

I saw nothing inside.

I hoped it was the exit. I relaxed against a wall. I took two breaths.

Suddenly images lit up on the walls, cinematic flashes from my mind's eye, all the images in my life, real images, like a woman walking in the rain across a bridge, a child cupping his hands to catch rose petals, a dog growling at me from behind a chain-link fence. Each image flashed on the black walls, detailed down to each blade of grass and the dew on the grass and the reflection of light and color in the drop of dew. There was too much, and if I were to write it down, it would take as much room as a library. I don't have enough time for that.

The first few days after visiting the library (after waking up), I walked around Tepotzlán in a daze. I have it mostly under control now, I think, but I can only keep sane by categorizing everything, and I find myself so exhausted from the work that I cannot walk anymore. I put each book and image and feeling and bit of knowledge (and emotions associated with them) into compartments, some of them secret, memories I never want to experience again. If the mystics are correct, and memories are what I will experience when I die, I want to live forever. No matter what manner of life I might have, I don't want to die. I cannot change the memories, because each one appears in detail. I won't leave my great aunt's house in Mexico. I won't get out of bed. There is no learning for me, only collecting and organizing. My great aunt brings me food to eat. I would thank her, but to talk is to recall all other times I've opened my mouth, to utter, to bite, to cry out for Nora.

22 HIDING PLACES

When they first moved into the old house, the boy imagined secret passages like a haunted house in the movies. You touch the bust of a statue, or you pick a book from the built-in bookshelf, or you pull the lever of a light fixture on the wall, and a secret door slides open. It reveals a winding stone staircase, which descends into a cold, dark room, a secret dungeon or laboratory.

All day and night the boy walked the hallways of the old house, through bedrooms and up the smooth, wooden stairs to the second floor, into more hallways lined by cold, empty rooms. He never found a secret passage, at least not like he had imagined, but he found his hiding places.

One was in his bedroom, in the closet, which was a better spot than one might think, because it was an old house and the closet floor had a trapdoor. He wished it led to some secret passage, some subterranean labyrinth lit by torches, but it was just a hole, a good hiding place nonetheless.

Upstairs, at the end of the hallway, in the ceiling, was a narrow staircase you pulled down with a rope. It was the entrance to the third-floor attic. From outside the house, the attic looked like a tower with a round window. From inside the attic — which his sisters never entered — the window looked out over the yard, a field of tall grass and yellow flowers, until it came to a line of pine trees and a dirt path that led to the river. He had hiding places two and three up there in the attic, one in the very back, opposite the window, behind a red-cherry chest of drawers that had belonged to someone before them. Even if someone came into the attic — which no one ever did — it would be hard to spot him in the darkness unless you shined a flashlight. The other hiding spot was in the rafters, behind a beam. He liked the attic in the late afternoon, when the sun shined directly into the round window — the wooden frame casting the perfect crosshair of a rifle across the wooden floor.

When they had moved into their new old house, his almost-teenage sisters complained that it looked too spooky. They hated the house. They said that they heard voices at night and that the walls seemed to pulse like lungs. In his bed alone at night he wanted so much to hear the voices, to feel the pulsing, but he didn't, and he felt that his inability to hear them was the ghosts' rejection of him, and it made him sad to be rejected by ghosts.

Four, five, and six were in the detached garage, seven was in the kitchen, under the cabinets, which was like a labyrinth, because he could crawl into various parts of the kitchen, including under the sink, where he liked to be hidden when someone ran the water. Eight was in the bedroom of his aunt and uncle, who had a secret door in their closet, but above, in the ceiling, which was hard to climb into. He had to stack up suitcases on a wardrobe chest to get up there. He could hear everything his aunt and uncle said to each other, the murmuring voices of the living, which wasn't very interesting. Nine and ten were in his sisters' bedroom, nine behind a heating vent, where through the slats he could see his sisters get ready for bed. Other hiding places were in various rooms, his aunt's sewing room, his uncle's pool room with a bar.

Number thirteen was in the anteroom, inside the big coat closet, behind the coats, a spot he liked best during winter, when cold radiated from the jackets. Four hiding places were in the different hallways, in linen and coat closets. One was behind the couch in the family room, from where he could hear his sisters gossiping and watching TV. Number nineteen was in the laundry room, adjacent to the kitchen, in a built-in shelf, where his aunt and uncle kept cleaning supplies, detergents and brooms and rat poison. Inside the shelves was a space small enough for a boy his size. One time he had hidden inside it while the family was in the kitchen eating dinner at the informal dining table. He could hear them calling for him, wondering where he had gone. "I hope he didn't go to the river," he heard his aunt say. "I hate that river."

"He's fine," his uncle said.

His aunt told his sisters to go look for him. They walked around the rooms of the house, calling for him, calling his name, their steps creaking on the floors and their disembodied voices echoing in the hallways. He giggled, and when they were a few feet away from him, he had to suppress his laughter or he would be found.

But his favorite three spots, places 20, 21, and 22 — the most incredible hiding places he had found — were on the outside of the house, on the other side of the cellar door. It was a double wooden door in the ground. His uncle had put a padlock on it, but the boy knew where to find the key. He cut a slab of wood into the door, his secret opening, so he could go in, remove the loose board, and stick out his arm to put the lock back on while he was still inside the cellar. The three hiding places inside were so wonderful that even if someone happened to go down there — where his family kept nothing — so why go down there? — they wouldn't be able to find him. They could shine a flashlight around, but they wouldn't see him. One was in the wall, a board that had come loose, creating a space just large enough to hold him, but very tightly. Another was under a built-in work table, behind a wooden crate.

But the best hiding place of all, number 22, was under a piece of plywood on the floor, as if the cellar had a cellar. The previous owners of the house — who knows which ones in the long line of owners? — had dug a hole, with a pickaxe it seemed, breaking through dirt and rock, maybe where they hid things. It was large enough to fit the boy. One day, he crawled into that cramped, cold space, slid the plywood over himself, and he fell into a deep sleep.

He was awakened by the sound of his sisters calling from above. He listened to their voices, calling him, shouting his name over and over, a name it occurred to him was not only his name. He suddenly felt the presence of another boy in the hole with him, or maybe a girl, one who had lived in the house years ago, a boy or girl now long dead, or maybe what he felt was the presence of someone not yet born, who would live in the house some day, a future boy with sun in his cheeks. The boy had no words for what he was feeling in that cold hole, just a sensation, a feeling that made him imagine he was already dead. He could see his spirit rising from the ground, passing through the twin cellar doors, into the sunlight, where he dissolved into specks of energy smaller than photons. He became the air his sisters breathed as they called his name, imagined himself the tiny particles floating down into their throats, into their centers, where he would cling for life to their hearts and lungs.

THE HOLY SPIRIT OF WINE

Un soir, l'âme du vin chantait dans les bouteilles:
Homme, vers toi je pousse, ô cher déshérité."
Baudelaire

He drank more than his share. I saw him from between the trees while I was pissing. I saw him looking to make sure I wasn't looking, and then he grabbed the bottle and drank from it like a man dying of thirst in a cartoon, a dried-up man crawling across the desert in rags, mouthing "Water! Water!" He gulped and gulped and put the bottle back on the ground, and when I came out of the trees, he stepped away from it and looked at the dirty wall of the museum, as if there were paintings hanging on the outside too. I was pissed. I picked up the bottle. His slobber was all over the bottle, white with phlegm, and I couldn't help it, I had to do something. Despite my living situation, I still had a taste for the finer things like wine, music, and art, and this wine was all I had. They wouldn't let me into the museum anymore — my clothes and smell — but I appreciated more than anyone the irony of us, poorest of the poor, making our camp under the trees, against the wall of the Museum of Fine Arts.

I knew it was my duty to give Rudy a chance to admit what he had done, because I believed in justice, and also, Rudy was one of my only friends, maybe because both of us — had we been born even one generation earlier — would have led quite different lives.

I decided that I would ask him if he had drunk my wine, and if he lied about it, I would do something to get him back.

When I brought the bottle to where he stood, he turned around to face me. He looked at the wine with lust. I held it up to the light that came through the trees from the avenue. We looked up to the bottle.

"How did you get it?" Rudy asked. The red wine swishing around the bottle reflected in his eyes. He was wearing some loose t-shirt, but his arms were so skinny that when they stuck out of his short sleeves it made him look naked, like an old man. He raised his arms, still looking at the liquid in the light, and he put his hands behind his head, his elbows jutting forward, and he clutched his hair in both hands, as if he wanted another drink so bad he might go crazy.

I told him how I had been walking through the cafes across from the plaza, when a waiter set a bottle of wine on a table and, forgetting his opener, went back inside the café to get it. At the same time, the customer who was going to drink the wine — a tall man with gray hair and a business suit — got a call on his cell phone. He stepped away from the table to go where he could hear better, and he talked with his back to the cafe. I walked by at that exact moment of grace, the perfect gift from god. I grabbed the bottle, shoved it in my pants and kept walking like normal.

Usually I drink whatever costs the least. I could work a few days collecting cardboard from garbage bags set out on the street, and I'd be able to buy wine so cheap it hurt to swallow but got me drunk. Yet this wine I was sharing with Rudy was a good one. It was smooth, velvety, with no aftertaste, and it came with a cork as well. When you broke the neck open on a rock, the Holy Spirit of Wine rose to your nose. I told Rudy I would share it with him, and I would have shared exactly half. Before I had gone to piss, we had been taking measured, fair drinks, and we were loving it, but when I went to piss, Rudy got greedy.

"Did you take a drink while I was gone?" I asked him.

Rudy looked shocked, his thin face caving in, his big eyes popping out.

He had bushy, expressive eyebrows that crawled up and down his forehead, rising now into caterpillar-arcs above his wide eyes. "Of course not!" He put his hand on his chest. "I swear to you. But let's have more. Let me have a drink."

He was a liar, I thought, as I took the next drink, certain I could taste the bitterness of his saliva in the wine. He would pay for what he had done.

I am measured and calm, always calm, and if there is anything obvious about me from a visual point of view, it would be how collected I am. The rage that I sometimes feel within me — and yes, this is what it's about, my inner rage — this rage that is rarely allowed into my language or behavior immediately races through my veins like electric liquid — and it shoots into my brain, where it becomes a thought. Over the years, I have devised in fantasy so many ways to kill so many people and get away with it, that if I were to write them down, they would sound like tales from Edgar Allen Poe. But I only allow myself to do this, that is, allow the rage to become a thought, because that way I never have to release it unwittingly through an uncontrolled burst of anger.

But handing Rudy the bottle, watching him take another drink, I knew I had to get back at him. I didn't think I would kill him, rather I thought that I would allow my thoughts to imagine a bloody death for him, when *in reality*, I would get revenge by giving him some tainted wine, something that would make him retch and vomit but wouldn't kill him.

I took weeks planning it, down to the last detail, but I also spent those same weeks thinking of the bloody version of the revenge, the fantasy revenge. Sometimes, I forgot which was which, and as I collected cardboard every night for a week, I entertained the violent thought too, that which I would have liked to do but wouldn't. I saved my money for a mildly toxic poison and a decent bottle of wine. I saw myself repeatedly hitting Rudy over the head with a full bottle of wine, until his head and the bottle busted open at the same time, the swirls of red warming my hands, which I would form into a cup and drink from, like ancestors drinking from a river. But of course, this was fantasy, the plan was only to poison him and laugh as he writhed in nausea.

When it came time to try my plan, I went to the Museum of Fine Arts, on our side, under the trees. A bunch of others were there, some sleeping in cardboard blankets or around their boxes of stuff, some sitting against the wall, some of them standing around a fire on the ground — inside a makeshift circle of rocks — drinking cheap wine. I asked them if they had seen Rudy, but there were three or four versions of where he had been spotted last. I stayed there around the fire, our shadows against the walls of the museum like the giant bodies of small gods.

When Rudy showed up, he was obviously drunk. He could barely walk, and when some young man passed by on a bicycle and yelled to him, "Get a job," Rudy ran after him, wobbling across the dark park like a zombie. He was yelling uncontrollably, stuff like, "You don't know shit about me!"

This was perfect, the perfect opportunity, a gift from god. I ran over to Rudy.

"Rudy, are you O.K.?"

He stumbled, looked at me, focused on my face, and then he recognized me. "That fucker!" he yelled. "Did you see that?"

"Yes, I know," I said. "Are you O.K.?"

"That fuck!"

"Terrible what he did to you," I said, very calmly. "I only wish we could catch up to him and teach him a lesson."

Rudy punched at the air, "I'll kick his ass!" He was slobbering. He kicked invisible enemies and stumbled and almost fell.

"Come on," I said, leading him away. "You're a good friend, Rudy. My best."

I knew I could exaggerate the language because he was drunk, and I really wanted to enjoy this. As we walked down the sidewalk, into the spotlight of a street lamp, I said, "You poor man. The victim of such verbal abuse. It's not fair! That rich brat doesn't know what a life you have."

"Asshole," Rudy yelled, and then he scrunched up his face, as if he would cry, but he was just getting the momentum in his facial muscles to yell again, "Let's see that bastard in my shoes!"

"He has no idea," I calmly said, leading him away. "You know what?" I asked. "I have some really good wine. Not cheap stuff, but the best. I stole it from an open window. Come on, I have it hidden, come with me and I'll share it with you."

I led him across the avenue, into another park, the one with the statues of the poets, and we walked by their dark gazes, Lorca, Quevedo, Dante, their eyes following us, and then we crossed a plaza busy with outdoor cafes, busy with people, music, lights. Young rich people hung out under the trees, children were begging from passersby, vendors sold flowers and balloons. Rudy was so drunk that he barely knew where we were going. "How perfect," I thought as I led him across the street into a narrow alley lined by tall buildings, the smell of the garbage like crushed, overripe grapes and motor oil. We walked into a labyrinth of alleys and narrow streets, until we got to the appointed place. It was another park, across the street from a main avenue lined by high-rise apartments. The park was closed at night, but I knew of an opening in the fence. I led him through the hole, into the trees, into the darkness.

It seemed like we were in a grove, an orchard of trees in the middle of the countryside, but the city groaned so painfully that you couldn't pretend it wasn't there.

I led him across the park, to the other fence, on the other side of which were miles of abandoned railroad tracks and rail yards. Further beyond the tracks were the shantytowns of poor families. Finally we reached the fence and stopped under a tree. No one would be able to see us. I pulled out the bottle and showed it to Rudy.

His eyes went wide and his eyebrows crawled happily up his forehead. "Wow," he said. "That's the same wine you had last time." He suddenly seemed sober. "You're going to share it with *me?*"

"You're my friend," I said. I held up the bottle, ready to break open the neck against the tree trunk so we could drink from the jagged end, but something overcame me. I felt the cold glass in my hand, and I couldn't remember which plan I was about to execute. I had planned on putting in the poison, which I had in my pocket, after I had a few sips, but now, feeling the bottle in my grasp, feeling that damn bottle, I wanted to kill him. I realized I had been planning on killing him all along. That had been my plan all along. Why else would I have had to bring him out there, where the chance of being seen was almost impossible? I held the bottle, ready to hit him on the top of the skull.

Rudy was so drunk that he couldn't hold up his head. He was looking at the ground, swaying back and forth, as if he would throw up. I was taller than him, and I could see the back of his greasy head. I lifted the bottle, and at that moment he fell to his knees. He began to weep, his shoulders rising up and down with his sobs.

"I stole your wine," he cried. "That night you shared it with me, I stole a drink. I'm sorry! You're the best friend I ever had. I'm sorry."

He was on his knees before me. "Forgive me. Please forgive me," he said. He grabbed my legs with his arms, and he pressed his head to my knees.

SARA'S CHEST OF DRAWERS

After Sara died, they told me to go through her chest of drawers, pick out what we might want to keep, and throw out the rest or give it away to charity. "Why me?" I asked, and they said it made more sense that way, since I knew her more intimately than anyone else did, since she was, in a sense, my other half.

"If Sara were looking over us right now," my mother said, "she would want you to be the one to go through her private things." My father, standing next to her, nodded his head in agreement, as if they had decided it together. We stood around in the sunlight of the kitchen.

"You never know," he said. "There might be something inside the drawers that could be embarrassing for her, some secret she had never spoken."

"We all have our things to hide," my mom said, "our secret stuff."

Dad shrugged his shoulders. He looked out into the backyard and sighed.

It was a cold, bright day in winter.

It struck me pretty hard: Sara with secrets. I had never thought about my sister's secrets, or that she would even have them, but I figured my parents were right, we all had them. I guess I even had some, and I guess if I were to die right now, there were/are a few items in my closet I may not want others to see. Nothing bad like pornography or drugs, but things that belonged only to me. I would feel violated if someone were to go into the corners of my closet and look for things.

So what would Sara have that was secret?

And if the dead can look at us, see us, watch our actions and maybe assert a little bit of energy into our world, what would Sara at that moment, standing in the kitchen with our parents, what would *she* want me to do? Would she want me to go through her chest of drawers, or would she want me to get a plastic trash bag, empty the contents without looking at them, and throw it into an anonymous dumpster somewhere in the city?

Now I felt with certainty that something more than underwear and socks, something terrible, was hidden in those drawers, and I felt that my parents knew it, too, and they wanted nothing to do with it.

Sara and I were different people, maybe even opposites, me the demon to her angel, although not that simple or obvious. We both had good qualities, we were both (I still am, I hope) decent people, but my dark edge was a little sharper than hers. I had a past, if you see what I mean, nothing that would get me arrested or kicked out of the house, but things that might make the average person uncomfortable to know about. Sometimes the light that came from the memory of my past shined dull in my eyes. It could make heavy my every movement, even the lifting of a fork to my mouth.

Sara on the other hand, spent her 22 years of life wheeling herself around the house, from window to window, all day long. She read poetry and novels or she listened to cello music playing in the other room. Any "private thing" of hers would have had to come out in her thoughts, because we never saw it or heard any hints of it. She mostly kept her words to herself, except for occasional meal-time musings, which were neither light nor dark, but kind of silly. One time we were all at the dinner table, and she looked out at the rose garden and said something about the night making itself hollow. I think it was "Shhhh. Listen to the sound of night making itself hollow." She was probably thinking about a poem she had read or one she was going to write. For the most part, when everyone was home, she was quiet in her bedroom. She never watched TV, but she listened to music, mostly symphonies, and she read books. The last time I saw her alive, I walked into the house when no one else was home. I saw her in her chair in the corner of the den, near a window, and she was reading a book. Some symphony was playing loudly, so she didn't notice me standing there watching her, for several turns of the pages. I was stunned by how old she looked, like she was eighty. When she looked up and saw me, she looked surprised, and then anger overcame her, as if I had walked in on her undressing. The shadow of the old lady fled from her face and body, and she became a radiant young woman, my twin sister, angry at me, almost beautiful in her indignation. Without saying anything, she wheeled her way into her bedroom, slammed the door and stayed in there, until days later, when the man and woman from the morgue removed her body.

The fact is, it took us about a week before we even knew she was dead, and she lived in the same house. It took the first three days for us to realize that she was quieter than usual. Mom must have knocked on her door 14 times, 7 for breakfast, 7 for dinner, but when Sara didn't come out, we simply assumed she didn't want to eat with us. We assumed she was in one of her dark moods.

I don't want to gross you out, but it was our dog Droopy that alerted us, smelling at her door, scratching and barking. We thought he was just going crazy, but then a few days later, we could smell it, too, feces and something else, like rotting vegetables, some stench coming from behind her door. On the seventh day, we opened it and looked inside. It was disgusting.

Now I sat on her bed. The room was tidy, the bed made with fresh sheets and good-smelling blankets, white pillows fluffed up like cherubs. I was looking at the chest of drawers, as if it were a coffin I had to open. It was a tall, wooden chest, an antique, the only piece of furniture Sara insisted on having. My parents had paid a lot for it one Christmas, but, boy, did it make Sara happy. I remember watching the light in her eyes as the delivery boys brought it in, this piece of furniture older than our home, its size made for a mansion, not a three-bedroom house like ours. They had to remove doors to get it into her bedroom.

I sat on her bed. I looked at the chest. It was very bright in her room, because all day mother kept Sara's curtains open, and she put fresh flowers on a small, round table near the window.

I counted twelve drawers. I closed my eyes, tried to feel the presence of Sara, but what came to me within my closed eyes was an image of her in her chair one late afternoon, rolling down the hall. I saw her reflection in the floors, rolling away down the hall.

I stood up, walked across the floor to the chest of drawers. "Sara?" I asked out loud. "What do you want me to do?"

That was when it happened.

I had been working at the same job for seven years. I was an assistant manager, so I'm not the kind of guy who would exaggerate the truth to tell a story. I don't even read stories.

Right after I asked my sister the question, "What do you want me to do?" the chest of drawers began to move.

I mean it really rattled, like a scene from *The Exorcist*. It rattled as if someone were inside of it, some raging spirit. The chest of drawers seemed to be saying, *"Get the hell away from me!"*

I took a step back. On a logical level, I knew the heating system in the basement had kicked on. It vibrated the floors of the house, like it did every time it kicked on. The vibrating floors in turn caused the chest of drawers to move, to rattle and shake. This is a fact of our house: For example, every time the heater kicked on and I was in my bedroom, it shook my bed, which had become a winter expectation. When I was a boy, I actually began to look forward to it.

The fact that the chest of drawers was moving was not the remarkable thing (that happened all the time); rather, it was the fact that it moved at the exact same time as I had asked the question. That couldn't have been random. What you have heard about twins is true, sometimes they can share thoughts and feelings even when they're not together. Sara had just died, so it was possible that her energy was still around. One of the basic rules of physics, the Law of the Conservation of Energy, states that energy cannot cease to exist, it simply changes form. People are energy, so it was possible that my sister's vibrations were still around as she was in the process of becoming another form, and that her energy could communicate with its twin energy, her brother. I took the movement of that chest as an answer about what I should do. I shouldn't look at her private things. She didn't want me to look.

But then something even stranger happened.

The heating system kicked on a second time. I don't know how that happened, how the heater had stopped and then started again in a matter of minutes. Usually it stayed on for hours, warming the house to the temperature set on the thermostat, and when it went off it stayed off for at least an hour before it needed to kick on again. But this happened within a matter of minutes. It kicked on again. I was facing the chest of drawers, and I heard something rattling behind me, like bones. I turned around and saw that the table by the window was vibrating. On top of it was a vase with fresh yellow flowers. The vase was shaking, rattling. The petals were moving.

Maybe it was the sunlight, maybe it was the exact yellow of the petals, but I suddenly felt my sister's presence. I felt her skin on my skin. I felt her enter my chest, fill me with her air, and I felt her face swell into the mask of my skin. She entered my thoughts. She wanted me to go through her drawers. She wanted me to see something. There was something among her private things that she wanted me to hold, and only me. I turned around and faced the chest of drawers. They looked so bright. I opened the first drawer.

THE DAY THEY DISCOVERED RAIN

The third bedroom of my uptown apartment sat empty, except for some boxes of old video cassettes spread around the floors. There was also a wobbly, wooden chair facing the three windows. The chair, which had belonged to my dead grandfather, was painted yellow, and that third room was always cold, because the windows, all three of them side by side, had those old wooden frames that you could pull up. Even when shut tight, the cold air seeped through, and sometimes, when it was windy, the air moaned.

I tried to keep that door closed, but the lock didn't always click, and at seemingly random times, the door creaked open and revealed the yellow chair facing the three windows.

One day, I decided to do something positive with that third room.

I'd convert it into a library.

How nice, I thought, to be able to come home from a long day at work, to plop my half-dead body on a leather armchair and read a good book, something classic, *Don Quixote, 1001 Nights, The Decameron*. I would read books on philosophy, science, art, anthropology, *The Origin of Species*, the Bible (though only for its historical value, having freed myself from cultural myth), the Koran, *The Interpretation of Dreams, Man and His Symbols*. As for collected works, I would have, of course, Plato, Dante, Homer and Shakespeare. I would have Neruda (preferably in the original Spanish, which I can read quite well with the aid of a dictionary) Kafka, Borges, Cortázar (the latter two also in Spanish), Molière (translated) and Walt Whitman.

I would also have every book ever published by Stephen King, including the titles under the Bachman pseudonym. I know that King is not considered "Great" by the makers of the canons, but this would be my library, so the books would not be according to anyone's opinion but my own. That said, I would feel no PC obligation to include ethnic or so-called Chicano writers.

One section of the library would be for intelligent magazines and literary journals, like *ZYZZYVA* and *The Harvard Review.*

In one corner of the room, there would be a roll-top desk made of solid oak, with legs like animal claws. On the desk I would keep two very big dictionaries, a Webster's English and a La Barron's English/Spanish.

One day, on my day off — after coffee and the morning news show — I visited the used book stores in my uptown neighborhood. As I walked into the tall, dark hallways of books — titles blurring by my peripheral vision like whispering voices, *The Plague, Cancer Bed, The Imaginary Invalid* — I realized that I was doing much more than converting the third room into something useful. I was changing my life.

I was finally going to overcome all that might have bridled me in the past: self-doubt, obsession with perfection. I had always wanted to be a reader of ideas, a connoisseur of words, maybe even some day I could be a creator of stories, a writer, maybe a poet. Ever since I was a child I felt that I was destined for something great, something big, and if I was ever going to discover what that was, this was the first step. As the titles blurred by — *The Last Mohican, The Wasteland, The Underground Man* — I realized that I, an intelligent, well-read young man, could create my own future. In creating my own private library I was, simply said, creating my freedom.

I found a matching set of hardback volumes of George Bernard Shaw, including *Candida*, *The Pygmalion*, and *Man and Superman*. At that same store, I also found a 1922 edition of tales by Edgar Allen Poe. The pages were of thick yet sheer paper, like onion skin, and each tale had woodcuts of dramatic moments. One sketch was positively horrifying: A beating heart pounds on the floor, while a frightened old man, surrounded by bewildered policemen, holds his own heart and screams in horror.

I couldn't wait to read the tale nor could I stop seeing that image in my mind for days (Therein lies, I thought, the power of great literature). The Shaw and Poe were together $122, which, I believe was well worth it.

At one used bookstore, the skinny clerk kept watching me from behind the counter, over her black-framed glasses. She had black hair and white skin and black lipstick and dangling earrings. She must have been curious about me, a young man spending Thursday afternoon looking through shelves of poetry. She must have thought I was a writer or a professor. Once, when I neared the bathroom, I caught sight of my image in an ornate but dusty mirror at the end of the hallway. My black hair was somewhat disheveled, scholarly looking, and my face had a stubble shadow. My black eyes shined with vision.

I piled books on the counter — some by authors I had never even heard of — Andrés Montoya, Lee Herrick, Agustín Porras. With one hand, the clerk opened the covers of each book to see the price inside written in pencil, and with the other, she entered the corresponding numbers into the cash register. Her thin fingers danced like a white spider across the keyboard of the cash register. She smelled like some floral body powder.

A few times, her eyebrows rose with approval at the stuff that I read (*would* read). That was when I noticed that she had purple eyes. Maybe they were contact lenses, but I liked the way they shined. I imagined asking her to help me carry the books home. My building was only a few blocks away. I was certain that the clerk would have been delighted to see my growing collection of hardbacks.

When the total was displayed, she looked out the window while I counted my money. She played with her hair, twisting it around her pointing finger. She wore black nail polish. I thought I heard her humming a tune, and her eyes were so stunning, so full of newness.

"It's a lot of books to carry home," I said.

Slowly, she turned her face away from the window. Her purple eyes looked at my face, then at my books, and then she looked out the window again.

That evening I made so many trips home with books — back and forth, up and down — with an energy I hadn't felt in years, sometimes singing some song as I ran up and down the stairs. I was sure the other tenants could hear, but I didn't care.

I still hadn't gotten the bookshelves, so I was forced to leave the tomes like orphans in the middle of the third room. I was too exhausted to sort them out, so I closed the door to that room, and I walked three blocks to Calhoun Square to get a pizza and rent a DVD. It was about a lunatic who kills people until an African-American psychologist talks to him, falls in love with his daughter, and makes him sane again. In one scene, the psychologist interviews the killer in some old prison, and the killer flat-out asks,

"Are you in love with my daughter?" Light comes through the stone window and shines on the killer's hands. For some reason, I thought of the girl at the bookstore, saying, "What a great camera shot. So much is being said through those hands!"

I imagined her next to me on the couch, leaning forward, watching the movie with me. A bowl of popcorn sat on her stomach. She looked at me, purple eyes sparkling, "I'm glad you got this movie."

Suddenly, a loud noise came from the third room.

The door slammed open. Wind was slapping the windows, the cold air coming into the room.

I got *The Decline and Fall of the Roman Empire*, *Mein Kampf*, *The Tibetan Book of the Dead*, and *The Island of Dr. Moreau*. At an antique fair in the Mall of America — a place I rarely went — I bought two boxes of *Life* magazines from the 1970s, with now dead people like Mohammed Ali and Richard Nixon on the covers. The expenditures for my library began to mount, and soon I spent my entire savings. The only cash I had was what remained at the end of each month from my paltry paycheck, so I figured it was time to hit the yard sales.

I had developed the skill of bargain hunting at a young age, because my grandfather was an aficionado of yard sales. He would drag me with him to the suburbs. He would talk the owners down so low on the prices that I almost felt sorry for them. They sadly held out their hands, in which my grandfather dropped coins. As we walked away from the sale, his face bitter, angry, he would mutter, "Those idiots don't know what they have."

Now in the Twin Cities, at yard sales and garage sales, I found mostly crappy and sappy books by people like

Sidney Sheldon and Harold Robbins, but I found a lot of Stephen King for a dime or a quarter.

Then one day, some man in St. Paul evoked something within me.

He lived in an old neighborhood near downtown. He smoked thin, long cigarettes in the dim corner of his detached garage. I thumbed through a hardback copy of *The Aztecs* by Gary Jennings. I had never heard of him or it, but it was about Aztecs, so it must have been good, I guessed, it must have been an important book. I continued to look through the pages, to make sure that they were all there, that there was no damage, but the man smoking his cigarette kept looking at me, as if I were going to steal something. I could only imagine what his racist mind must have been thinking about me. I'm a Latino man, you could even say a Chicano. He saw me holding a thick, black book that said *AZTECS.* He was probably afraid I was going to steal it.

I became enraged.

I wanted to say something, to do something.

I fantasized taking him back to my place. I'd drag him up the stairs and open the door to the library — wood and leather gleaming in sunlight — and he could see for himself the kind of man I was.

I spent the next few weeks away from my library project, having temporarily closed the door, as it were, to the third room. The pile of books looked like a pyre, ready for one of those book burnings that narrow-minded fanatics from time to time impose upon culture. I could see my copies of *Daniel Deronda, Tom Sawyer, Ana Christie,* all aflame, their hard backs twisting, bending with the melt, the skin shriveling up. I tried to keep the door to the third room closed, but when the wind picked up, it kept opening.

I had inherited my grandfather's yellow chair when the extended family, shortly after he died, swarmed through his house carrying away whatever items they suspected might be valuable, which they shoved into their SUVs. I arrived in California from Minnesota. I pulled up to his house in a rental car. Most of the relatives were driving off with their loot, few of them courteous enough to wave at me or to roll down their windows to say hello. I got the very last choice of what to take, which turned out to be a rusted carving knife that I now used to open letters, and the yellow chair in the third room. I hated my family for that treatment of me. I had known him better than all of them. He raised me. I remember sitting for hours at the kitchen table while he drank instant coffee or talked on the phone with idiot bill collectors or idiot family members. He used to hit me when he ran out of cigarettes, as if I had been the one smoking them. I should have gotten first choice.

I arrived late to the wake, so most of the family members were already walking to their cars. They looked furtively at me as I walked into the arched entrance of the nave, but most just ignored me, like I was spit. I walked down the middle aisle lined by dark wooden pews — I could smell the waxy candles that flickered by my vision — to the open coffin before the altar, under the lights. The top half was open, the inside lid lined by satiny white like a halo around his head. I was shocked by what I saw.

His old face had a large grandfatherly smile, because the embalmers had shaped away his bitter eyes, molded off his evil smirk. The dead man in the box — the old man with face makeup and a manmade smile — was not my grandfather, was not the man who used to grab my forearm with both his hands and twist my skin in opposite directions, an Indian Sunburn, he called it, until it burned so bad my eyes shut with pain. This man in the coffin was what a grandfather *should* have been. It enraged me to think that this man who lay before me, this bitter monster at my waist, could evoke sympathy. They could come in here and see his dead face and be fooled into thinking he was a fucking sweet old guy. I turned around and looked to the entrance. No shadows, no voices.

I grabbed his hand and lifted it to my chest. It was cold.

"Bastard!" I told him. "You phony bastard."

I bent back a finger until I heard it snap, and then another and another. I grabbed his skinny arm in my two hands and snapped the bone. I would have done a lot more, but I felt shadows fill the entrance of the nave. I turned around.

Two funeral workers stood in the archway.

"Oh, sorry," said the tall one, standing in chiaroscuro.

"No problem," I said. "Just saying goodbye to abuelo."

One morning, I walked to Calhoun Square and had coffee, not cheap chain-store coffee, but good thick coffee at a place where they grind their own beans. I sat near the storefront window. Kids dressed in leather and with spiky hair walked by on the sidewalk.

The skinny bookstore clerk with the purple eyes came into the coffee shop. She stood in line at the counter. She had a black book bag, which hung heavy from her shoulder as she waited for her order. Her dangling earrings, each one a tree on a hill, slightly swayed from her ears. After she was served, she set her bag and latte on the table across from me. She pulled out a thick volume of what appeared to be the collected works of Shakespeare. She lifted the foamy latte to her black lips and sipped. She turned the pages to where she had left a bookmark. She began reading. She wore a black sweater and tight black pants, and she was very skinny. She wasn't pretty by conventional means, her skin was blotchy, pimply, but that didn't matter to me. What attracted me to a woman was something more. Something deeper, intellectual, spiritual. I was ready and willing to meet the right one.

Since the girl was so absorbed in her book (a sign of good character) I knew that I would have to initiate contact. I ran phrases through my mind that might stimulate intelligent conversation. I decided that it would be best to approach her in a way that addressed her social function as a bookseller. I wanted her to trust me, not to think I was some lovesick boy who might follow her everywhere, like a derelict dog you had to throw rocks at so he'd go away.

So I rose from my seat, and with a cup of coffee and trembling confidence, I approached her table. My shadow slowly spilled over the white pages of her book. She looked up at me with pale, lavender eyes.

"I'm sorry for intruding," I stuttered. I suddenly felt like an idiot, as if I wasn't the kind of guy to have his own library. "We met before. I don't know if you remember."

She looked as if she didn't recognize me (a smart step for a single young woman in the city).

"I was in your bookstore a few weeks ago. I bought a lot of poetry books."

She squinted her eyes against the sun. Her face was ghost white, except for the rose-colored blotches of acne. I didn't know what I was going to say next, so I focused on her earrings, the tree on the hill.

"What's up?" she said.

"I couldn't find any poetry by, uh. . ."

I knew the name I was about to say had to be of a great writer, yet someone only the few knew about, only those who truly loved poetry. I hadn't yet had a chance to read anything, so I made up a name that I hoped sounded like a great poet. "Uh, any books by. . . uh, François Norbert? Do you know if any of his books have come in?"

She shook her head and said, "I don't know."

"Well, I was just wondering. He's a great poet, isn't he?"

"I'm on break," she said.

"I'm starting a library," I said. "My own private library."

"That's great," she said and then she looked back at her book.

"What library is complete without François Norbert, right?" Out the window, a homeless black man wrapped in a blanket held out his hands to the white, young passersby.

The girl was reading.

"I think. . .of course that his best work is *The Day They Discovered Rain.*"

"What's that?" she said, suddenly interested.

"The Day They Discovered Rain."

"That's a great title," she said.

"He's great," I said, flattered that she liked the title.

"Well, I better get back to my book," she said.

"How does that one poem go?" I said, pretending to recall and recite something that had never been written:

> *On the blue curve of earth,*
> *they held up their arms and felt falling*
> *water on their palms, their faces*
> *and they laughed like children laugh.*

"That's nice," she said.

"I see you're reading the Bard," I said. "Are you a student?"

"I'm a student," she said.

"Ah, Shakespeare!" I said. "A great man, too. Like Norbert."

"I'll have to read him," she said, kind of smiling, but it was kind of crooked, like a teenager trying to hide her braces.

Miss Dulwater, who used the desk next to mine, told me where I could get a good deal on barrister's bookshelves, the kind with the glass doors, three of them, tall and stately, and very sophisticated looking. "You want a nice library, these bookshelves look classy."

I sat before my computer, entering credit card number after number *–4138-6334*. She stood up, sat at the edge of my desk, and crossed her legs. She looked up at the lights, as if they might help her think. "What was her number?" she asked herself, while I was typing in more and more numbers — *5563-9998*.

"Oh, yes," she said.

She uncrossed her legs, reached for a pen on my desk and leaned in close to me. "Do you mind?"

7765-3338

She wrote down the phone number of the owner.

"She's a really old lady," said Miss Dulwater. She handed me the piece of paper. I stopped typing numbers and tried to take it from her, but she didn't let it go right away. "She's like a nice old grandmother," she said. "Go see her before she croaks."

I spent that weekend mostly at home, with no furniture for my library, so the door remained closed. I drank coffee, watched TV, rented DVDs and even bought some episodes of a sitcom I used to watch when I was a teenager. After watching four or five episodes, I got bored with TV, so I gathered some change from my pants pockets and couch cushions and walked to Calhoun Square and sat at the bar at BBQ and Blues. I bought a beer and listened to the blues. The place was packed with people, couples and groups, laughing and talking, and there I was squeezed in on the only empty bar stool. I wondered if the girl who worked at the bookstore liked the blues. I pictured her standing next to me, my arm around her waist, and she raised her beer mug for a toast. "I love the blues," she said.

"They're so honest," I said.

"Yeah, *honest*," she said.

The next day I woke up feeling heavy. I looked out the living room window onto the tree-lined street of my uptown neighborhood — old mansions converted to condos and apartments, old-fashioned streetlamps shaped like giant candles. It was cold, a slight drizzle of snow, another season of my life, another winter.

I called the lady with the bookshelves and got directions to her house near one of the city's lakes. It was one of those old Victorian mansions. An old woman opened the door. She led me into a musty anteroom with red velvet chairs on either side. The lighting was poor. She smelled like mothballs, like the inside of my grandfather's closet. I remembered hiding inside of that closet, dark and musty and smelling of mothballs and bug spray. I would listen for my grandfather's footfalls on the hollow floors as he looked for me. I remembered the wind-whipping sound of the switch he had torn off the weeping willow.

"This way," the old lady said. Her old, hunched figure disappeared into a room. We reached a hallway lined with paintings and chairs which cast shadows across our path. Lamps hung over the pictures, faces of the dead, stern old men in military uniforms, ladies with tall hairdos and gold broaches. She was so small and feeble, walking so tentatively, the shadows of her limbs created a crystal cathedral which trembled on the walls.

I could have been some demon she had let into her home, could have hit her over her white head with a brass lamp, could have watched as the blood splayed down the sides of her head. I could have sliced her into pieces with my grandfather's broken carving knife, which I had used earlier to open mail and unconsciously had slipped into my back pocket. It was still there. I could feel it. On holidays when my grandfather used it, I was a small boy, pressed against the wall, protecting my ears and gaze from the buzzing knife and the embittered look in his eyes as he carved the bloody chunk of meat, as his children — my aunts and uncles — waited with their empty plates raised, on which he slapped a slab. Only he was allowed to cut the meat, only he was allowed to give it out.

The old lady led me to a wooden staircase. She walked up with much effort, opening the door into the light of a dusty den, the likes of which I had only seen on TV. The room smelled of stale pipe tobacco and bad breath. But what stood before me, in the center of the room, were three strong wooden boys, chests out. I tried to feign aloofness, but a moan slipped out of my mouth, and the old lady, looking at me with greedy eyes, said, "They're very nice, aren't they?"

She also had a roll-top desk, with clawed feet, just like the one I had pictured for my library. For the three shelves and the desk she wanted three thousand dollars. I fantasized throwing her to the floor and tying her up and stuffing her into a closet, but it wasn't a very good fantasy. How would I explain to the neighbors and to whomever I had to hire to help move the shelves the absence of the old lady? Fantasies that could never truly happen were not worth dwelling on. The following day, I went to the bank, took the money out of a credit card — and a hundred extra to have someone deliver them — and I paid the old lady in hundreds, which she slipped into her smock pocket. She agreed to have them delivered the next day. When I left her house, I was too full of energy, too full of hope, so I didn't go home.

I went to the Mall of America, the biggest indoor mall in the country, the epitome of consumer culture. There were four levels of stores like Old Navy and Sak's Fifth Avenue and The Minnesota Store, where they sold stuffed moose and T-shirts that said "You Betcha!"

In the middle of the mall, in a giant glass atrium, an amusement park rose to the artificial sky like a carnival nightmare, a park filled with hundreds of people. It smelled of cotton candy, and a person in a Snoopy suit walked around and shook hands with kids as their parents took photos. Rollercoasters reached into the air and clanked and squealed like metal monsters, and people screamed as their metal boxes clanked down the tracks. I walked past the Ferris wheel, through the crowd, and into another section of the mall. On the main floor a spaghetti bowl of escalators crisscrossing the sky surrounded me. Glass elevators framed in gold slid up and down to the dome ceiling. The Revlon company had set up a fashion show stage and a walkway. Skinny teenage girls in tight clothes walked up and down while thousands of onlookers gawked, from all levels, even at the very top floor, where they held onto the rails and looked down onto the stage.

I walked faster, past Barnes and Noble, past CD stores and JC Penney and into Macy's. I must have been walking like a man with determination, because people got out of my way. Unlike those who wanted to shop, who allowed themselves to be seduced by images and smells, I was on a mission.

I found the Macy's furniture section, and that was where I saw it:

My dream chair.

An oversized leather armchair with ottoman.

I sank into it. So comfortable. So soft and firm. Never in the history of chairs was there one more comfortable. The price was $2800 for the chair and $1580 for the ottoman, a total of $3,380. A high price to pay for sure, so the doubts began to flood over me, but I remembered movies that I had seen where libraries and studies were elegantly furnished. This was what I wanted. It was time to start my life. I'd throw out my grandfather's old yellow chair.

The salesperson, a thin boy with a thin tie, came up to me as I was sitting in my chair. He looked me up and down.

The carving knife in my back pocket poked my lower back.

"Can I help you?" he asked.

I looked up at him, put my feet on the ottoman. "Yes, you can, young man," I said. "You could ring up this chair for me."

"And the ottoman?" he said.

"Of course."

I spent that evening and the next morning clearing the books out of the soon-to-be library, to get ready for the furniture-delivery people. I had to pile books all over the apartment, in the extra room, my bedroom, on my bed, in the living room — a stack on the TV and on the coffee table and on my eating table and all over the hardwood floors.

When the guys came with the bookshelves, they had to step over the piles. Once the shelves were in, they brushed off their hands and looked around.

"You got a lot of books," one guy said.

"I once knew somebody with lots of books," the other guy said, looking around.

Next, two other guys came with the chair from Macy's. I had the boys place it in the middle of the library. They said nothing, just looked around and had me sign the papers. I looked down on the yellow painted chair, so wobbly and weak, and I said, "I guess I won't be needing this anymore."

Where it came from, I didn't know, but I grabbed the yellow chair and violently threw it out the library door and watched it roll into the middle of my living room. "I hate that chair," I said.

The Macy's delivery boys looked at me, looked at each other, and they left.

First, I placed books on the shelves, not according to any logical order, just by how they looked, hard volumes next to volumes of the same size. I figured it would be better to get the books on the shelves and then to organize later, a job that might very well take a long time, maybe years, considering that I worked full-time and would have to organize my library during my spare hours. It would be my project, my vision, my quest, and it was exciting. I was happy. The books, the leather Macy's chair, the antique desk, the barristers bookshelves, they all looked so extraordinary, just like I had pictured, maybe better.

But then a problem arose.

The bookshelves could only hold what books I had stacked in my bedroom. They were completely full, yet books were still piled up all over the apartment. It depressed me somewhat, because that meant I would need twice as many bookshelves, not all of which would fit in the library. I would perhaps have to use other rooms. Then I thought, yes!

It would be like having an entire apartment-library. I walked into the extra bedroom. As I said, there were three bedrooms in the apartment. I imagined myself knocking down the wall that separated the extra room rom my library.

But for now I was happy.

The library looked great, wood and leather. Sunshine flooded in from the three windows. The leather armchair in the sun was a burnt orange color, almost yellow.

I sat and put my feet on the ottoman.

I felt such peace come over me.

I knew for sure it was worth the expense, even if it took me years to pay off, to organize, to get it exactly right, it was my own library, my own private library!

I fell asleep on the armchair and dreamed of wind blowing through the three windows, lifting the sheer white curtains. I stood at the windows looking out onto a city of books, books as far as the eye could see, books, not buildings, some of them sky scrapers. The tallest book downtown read across the spine *The Day They Discovered Rain*. It began to rain, soaking the books, the black liquid of ink running off the pages and flowing into the gutters.

I grew up in a part of California where rain was rare and welcomed, yet I cannot remember the first time I discovered it. I cannot remember the first time I felt its wet on my skin or the very first time I stood in the frame of a window and watched the rain wet the grass. All I remembered was how I stood as a child, whenever it rained, at the window, watching the water fall on the lawn, on a stone bench, on cars parked on the street. I felt sorry for things, for all things, a kid's ball on a lawn, a bicycle leaning against a stone fence, because everything was getting wet, everything was cold and sad. I wanted to bring things in from the rain, and one time I did, piling sundry items in the middle of my grandfather's living room, cracked red pots, a child's dump truck, a wagon with three wheels. My grandfather came in and saw the stuff, and he made me throw the things back outside, unprotected in the rain.

When I woke up, I felt sad. It was Saturday night. I decided to cheer myself up with pizza and a movie. I walked the three blocks to Blockbuster and rented a DVD.

STANLEY GOTO, STORY DETAIL CATALOGUER

I was writing a story about a furniture delivery man who has dreams of becoming a great opera singer, but he can't carry a tune. No matter how hard he tries, he's the worst singer ever, so he has to content himself with delivering furniture for the rest of his life. One day, he twists his ankle while he's mowing his backyard, and he subsequently loses his job. A week later, his young wife dies in a car accident. After days of grief so intense that the ex-furniture delivery man cannot physically function, he is visited by an angel who grants him the most beautiful singing voice ever, a voice with which he can express his grief, a voice that'll make people weep. The angel, a brown woman with round brown eyes that pop out, like an iguana, warns him that the sad beautiful voice is his for only a year, in which time he must get over his grief and then go on to do good things with his life. For the first three months after the angel's visit, the widower hardly even speaks aloud, believing that the angel with the iguana eyes was a dream. Every day and week that pass he grows weaker in his grief, and he begins to feel a great stinging pain in his side and suspects that, like his mother and father before him, he has cancer. He wants to sing out, to fall on his knees and release the pain, but he is convinced that he can't sing. He created the angel in his mind, down to the last detail: iguana eyes.

One night, over eleven months and several weeks after the death of his wife, he gets drunk in a small downtown bar. It happens to be karaoke night. The ex-furniture delivery man is drunk, and he remembers the angel. Suddenly, he imagines that she sits on the bar stool next to him. She says, "Sing. You must sing."

He grabs the binder which lists the songs, thumbs through it and then writes letters and numbers with a pencil on a note pad, and he hands it to the bartender, but when he turns around, the angel is, of course, gone.

When it's his turn, he gets up from his stool and walks across the bar to the microphone in front of the dance floor. He is going to sing REM's "Losing My Religion."

He holds up the microphone to his mouth, and sings.

Oh, Life!   It's bigger
It's bigger than you   and you
are not me

His voice cracks so beautifully, like crumbling stone.

I thought that I heard you laughing
I thought that I heard you sing.

Bar patrons start crying, everyone does, even the cocktail waitresses as they walk across the floor with trays over their heads and the bartenders as they pop open beer bottles. When the song is over, everyone in the bar is silent, as they bathe in the afterglow of sadness. The ex-furniture delivery man begins to cry, too, not because the song was so sad, but because he knows that it has been a year's time since the angel visited him, and tomorrow, he will wake up and not be able to sing.

I liked the story, but after writing it, I wasn't sure about some of the details. Before, whenever I wasn't sure of an image, I consulted my friend Stanley Goto. He was a Story-Detail Cataloguer, one of the few who could make a living at it. He had a long list of famous clients who wouldn't dream of having a book published until he took a look at it. I won't mention any names, but let me say that a certain Indian-British novelist wouldn't publish a word without Stanley's consultation.

I had met him in grad school, in the fiction MFA program. He was of Japanese descent, quite smart, and he was a good writer, too, the darling of the program. One day Stanley and I were riding our mountain bikes in the hills outside of campus, going down the trails so fast that the world vibrated in my vision like a hand-held camera during an earthquake. At a sharp turn in the path, Stanley's front tire hit a rock, and he flew over his handlebars and hit the ground pretty hard. Even though he was wearing a helmet, the impact of his head was pretty severe. I was about a hundred feet behind him, but I could still hear it, so loud, a thump. He lay there, and I thought he was dead.

After the accident, after the brain surgery, he couldn't write fiction, because he had no sense of creativity. He had lost his ability to imagine. Somehow, he had expanded the part of his brain that recalls information. He became like a computer. I remember one time standing in awe when I dropped a box of cereal and he told me exactly how many flakes had fallen out, and he could tell me the exact position of each one of them even after I had cleaned them up. Instead of becoming a fiction writer, what he most desperately wanted to do, he started spending all his time reading books of fiction and literary journals, everything you could imagine from *1001 Nights* to *In The Grove*, a litmag out of Fresno, California. He remembered absolutely every detail he read. He figured that he might as well do something with his new talent, so he started helping writers by reading their work. He traced all of their images, all of their detail, to earlier sources, so they could know what was trite, so they could know how often an image they had created had been created by someone else. It's no secret that writers unconsciously store striking details in books we read, and then these details sometimes come out when we're writing, without remembering where we got the idea. There are some cases when writers have written entire books, just to later realize that they have rewritten a book they had read before. I once knew a writer in the MFA program who worked on a novel for five years, only to learn after it was all done that he had rewritten Chang Rae Lee's *Native Speaker*.

I once wrote a story with a detail that went, "The pool looked as if it had swallowed the moon." The pool was in the center of the apartment complex, separating the protagonist's window from a single mother who lived in the apartment across the way. At night when the sky turned black and the underwater pool lights snapped on, blue light glowed on the wall of her building. "It looked as if the pool had swallowed the moon."

I called Stanley and read him the story. When I got to the image of the pool swallowing the moon, Stanley grunted. "What is it?" I asked.

Without even having to look it up in his computer database of prose images, the largest in the world, which he was about ready to publish in a ten-volume set, *Detail Catalogue for Fiction Writers*, also to be available in electronic format — he said to me, "That particular detail came pretty late, in 1973 with Danny Malvid's novel *The Way of the Sidewalk*, basically a suburban adultery guilt thing about a man living alone in a big white house, empty because his family left him. The only thing that remains of his family is a rubber dinosaur floating in the pool in the backyard. 'The rubber dinosaur glowed on the water, as if the pool had swallowed the moon.'"

"Although that was the first known use of that detail," Stanley told me over the phone, "you could argue that the detail first appeared in creative literature–in a different form, of course — in 450 BC with the Greek poet Gronk. He wrote a comedy called *The Butterflies,* where a deity stands in a puddle after a heavy rain flooded the city. He looks at his feet and says, 'My ankles disrupt the moon,' which amounts to the same thing, yes?"

Depending on what Stanley Goto told me about an image, I kept it or discarded it. Details which worked only on a narrative level — those which didn't contribute somehow to theme or metaphor and archetypes — were easy to discard in revisions, but when I was writing a story and the detail seemed to fit on all levels, including language (rhythm and sound), I was reluctant to give it up.

I liked the story about the furniture delivery man, but before I sent it out to a journal, I gave Stanley a copy to read. He suggested that I replace REM's "Losing My Religion" with another song, as it had been used several times in the last few years in published fiction. The first case was in an obscure literary magazine out of Eugene, Oregon, a journal called *Hole in the Mountain Review.* The story was about a boy who goes with his friends to pre-Katrina New Orleans for Mardi Gras. He loses them and ends up by himself the entire weekend, lonely, wandering the cemeteries and the French Quarter. The streets are packed with people in beads and costumes and the smell of beer. Music blares from the window of a balcony: "Losing My Religion."

Stanley said that from the release of the song in 1989 all the way to October 2006, five other uses of "Losing my Religion" appeared in fiction, the last one in *BorderSenses,* a journal started by graduate students in El Paso, Texas. I was reluctant to give up the detail for my story, because it fit so well into the theme of the tale, since it was about — at least on one level — the loss of the ex-furniture delivery man's roots: his wife, his job, his comfort, his faith in life, his — by any other name — religion. I also thought that the name "REM" worked on the level of motif, since it is indeed the time (rapid eye movement) during sleep when one is most separated from present reality, and thus, the time for dreaming. I was determined to keep the detail.

Stanley, however, reminded me of the curse of Zoltan Olan.

The curse is similar to any curse based on a number, like the American president curse, which people believed years ago. The curse predicted that a US president elected in a year that ended with "00" would be assassinated or, like in the case of Ronald Reagan, would at the very least be shot. But the Zoltan Olan curse has never, Stanley assured me, suffered an exception. When he had first told me about it, I thought it sounded a little crazy, but I recalled that Stanley had no imagination, so it must have come from somewhere.

Zoltan Olan was a book repairer in Houston, Stanley said, inarguably the best book repairer in the world. Even at a time when other book repairers had gone out of business, the field becoming a dying art, Olan's little storefront workshop in downtown Houston thrived with jobs from all over the world. It wasn't unusual for national libraries, from Paris to Addis Ababa, to send their most prized ancient texts to Olan, books which threatened to disappear under decay. Olan did the best work. He could bleach pages so that they didn't look whitewashed. He kept the letters naturally dark, but at the same time the pages kept the yellow tint of age. Some believed that he was working on a chemical solution that would have stopped acrylic-based ink from fading off the pages of a text after hundreds of years, which was of course how so many important books had been lost. No one knew how close he was to achieving this goal, but everyone knew that if anyone could have solved this problem, it would have been Zoltan Olan.

So many priceless books passed through his hands that it wasn't unusual to see Secret Service agents — wires to their ears — hanging out in front of his downtown shop. Olan took on an assistant, who later would go on to be a book repairer for Harvard University, offering classes in the art of book repair, a young Italian Jew who came to Houston from the Bronx specifically to apprentice under Zoltan. The books were often priceless, but Zoltan Olan didn't care about money. He lived for his work, his art.

One day a book arrived that Zoltan loved so much that he took twice the time to do the work, just to be in its presence. Only about twelve hundred years old, it had seemingly normal qualities. It was written in German. The cover was made of wood and a strip of leather near the binding. Like a lot of books that age, the wood had tens of tiny holes where worms had bored in over the centuries. The most amazing things about the book, however, were the woodcuts. These images, each of which contained the signature of the artist, SG, illustrated the death and resurrection of Christ,

The illustrations were like none he had never seen. In one image where Christ hangs on the cross, he smiles as the Romans stick a spear in his side. The blood that flows from the wound, if you examine it closely, is letters flowing from the body, the first time Olan had seen such a detail in any book. Olan then noticed something else.

In the rest of the book, that particular detail appeared seven times, blood as language, or rather, blood as letters, but so subtly you had to examine the image closely, and only then could you see the tiny *T*s and *S*s and *P*s flowing from a wounded Christ. Zoltan read the text for an explanation (he could read in ten languages), but found no reference to blood as flowing letters, and he looked everywhere for information on who the artist might be, but he found nothing.

This book belonged to the German government, a valued treasure that they finally reclaimed from a secret order of monks living in an abbey among seven snowy mountains. One day the book was missing from Zoltan's storefront shop.

Some suggested that the young assistant had taken it, but that proved to be impossible. Shortly afterwards, as Zoltan Olan, the only logical suspect in the case, was being investigated by three governments, and after his book collection, one of the most amazing private collections in the world, had been seized, the book repairer was found murdered. Execution style. A bullet in his forehead.

That was all that was ever heard about the case until the summer of 2001, when a flood came to Houston, causing disaster to many buildings and parks and at least one cemetery. History says that Zoltan's coffin spit up out of the earth, swished atop the rapid water, out of the cemetery, onto the freeway, and it smashed against a brick wall. His dusty remains spilled out. Later, spotted at night in the water's reflection of the moon, were the floating pages of the missing book.

Now Stanley told us that the Zoltan Olan Curse said that whenever a particular detail was used in published fiction for the seventh time, something bad would happen to the writer. For example, after the seventh use of the pool swallowing the moon detail, the writer not only got the story rejected 67 times, but after a small journal in Adams County, Ohio — edited by a high school astronomy teacher — published the story, the journal went under and a year later the writer died of pneumonia. Another writer, a very famous writer (whose name I won't mention), was said to have used seven such cursed details in a single novel, and he had such bad luck that some people in some parts of the world put a death threat out on him, and he became one of the most hated figures in the world. Now he was one of Stanley's clients.

So despite how perfect REM's "Losing My Religion" would have been in the story about the ex-furniture delivery man, I changed the song to Led Zeppelin's "Going to California," which had metaphorical qualities of its own.

According to Stanley, the "Going to California" detail had been used 1,798 times in the last three decades, but the reference to the song by Led Zeppelin had appeared only three times, two in obscure publications and once in *The New Yorker*. Thus it was O.K. to use it as a detail, "Quite safe," he assured me.

THREE

THE MAGIC DUCK

I am a duck. I can't help it if my feet flap as I waddle, and my beak is kind of round and wide, that's just me. That's duckeditity. I do nothing to earn the money that the man in the yellow sweatpants collects sitting in the plaza. He sits on a blanket. He's a big brown man the size of a VW Bug, which is what he drives. He's so big that he had to take out the backset so he could fit in the driver's seat, and he has to lean forward as he drives, his nose practically touching the windshield, so his head doesn't hit the roof. He drives with the window down, and sometimes he sticks his head out the window and feels the wind blow on his face and through his long hair. He puts me and the stuff of our trade in the passenger's seat. He doesn't put me in a cage, which is good, because I hate cages. He's not worried that I'll fly away, so even when he walks across the plaza to set up for the day — for the thing I do to make our living — I am free. I follow behind him. People watch us and they think it's cute. I've heard that so many times, *How cute!* that the words cease to mean anything to me. They are just sounds, like what quacks must be to humans.

I walk behind him always, even when he goes across the street to the liquor store. He knows I won't fly away, because where would I go? I don't know where I came from. I only have one vague memory of my past. I see a body of water, maybe a lake or a pond, and me and a bunch of other baby ducks are quacking and squawking and walking behind some big female duck through some trees, but other than that I have no identity as a duck. Sometimes I'm not even sure if it's my memory or if it was something I saw on TV, some Disney cartoon maybe.

In fact, I have to keep saying to myself, "I'm a duck. I'm a duck." Sometimes I forget that fact. For a long time I thought I was dog. He fed me with the other dog. We ate cans of dog food, little cans of minced meat that he put on paper plates on the floor of his apartment. As I ate, the man in the yellow sweatpants sat fatly at the table eating a bowl of cheesy meaty stuff, using a wooden spoon as big as a fairy tale spoon. I pecked at the minced meat on the paper plate, and if the little dog came anywhere near me while I was eating, I would flap my wings and run in to attack him. I thought I was a dog, but as I reflect on it now, I don't think that the real dog, that tiny white thing, concerned himself much with my identity — a duck or a dog? — because he was too preoccupied with getting enough to eat. All I was to him was "the other," the one who prevented him from getting what he wanted. He ended up running away. I guess he wasn't happy with me and the man in the yellow sweatpants, and who could blame him? He wasn't a very good fighter. I'd peck at him and he'd cry and hide all day in the closet. I sometimes wonder where he went, picturing his little legs running through alleys and across parking lots, looking for food, looking for someone to take care of him. Frankly, I admire his bravery, the sheer courage of what he did. I dream of doing it too (or I *have* dreamed), but a duck walking through the alley of the inner city might draw more attention than a little white dog.

The fat man in the yellow sweatpants takes me to the plaza each day, unless he's tired from too much food and booze or he's too depressed to get off the couch where he sleeps. We arrive at the plaza, and he puts down his blanket. He plays music on a small tape player, some circus music, stupid sounds if you ask me, notes on instruments that lose their potential to move me because of their harmonic relationship to each other. Ducks — if I dare speak for all ducks — prefer seemingly chaotic sounds. Artistic form, especially for music, is when a work allows the listener to make predictions about what rhythms will come, and to be correct about it; but in the work of genius, that is, a work of perfect form, the predictions we are allowed to make are both satisfied and subverted. Good music surprises us with its movements, but the surprises come from the work itself.

Therefore, the sound of nature is perfect music, and since music is the purest form of art, nature is perfect in itself. Of course, I'm only saying what everyone else already knows. My point is that the music that the man in the yellow sweatpants played on that little box sounded like little geometric shapes, balls bouncing off each other in predictable and redundant patterns.

He starts the pathetic music, and then he puts me in front, and he sits on the blanket. There is a sign he made that says "See the Amazing Magic Duck." All I do is stand there watching the passersby, and for some reason, they find me amusing. They say those words over and over, *How cute! How cute!*, and they put coins and paper money into the coffee can. The man in the yellow sweatpants taught me to walk over to the can every time I hear money fall into it. I do the same thing every time: I look into the can. I stick my beak far into it, and then I quack with my head still inside, which makes the sound kind of tinny and echoey. I guess that's what makes me a magic duck.

Sometimes I think I'm human. This happens especially those nights when he and I are alone in his apartment. He gets depressed and drinks whisky and eats microwave burritos that he buys and heats up at the liquor store across the street. The Arab boys know him there, and they know me, too. Sometimes he takes me with him. I follow him inside the double doors. The store clerks say stuff about health department rules, but then they laugh when I waddle up to them. They give me pieces of candy.

Anyway, those nights when he gets so depressed that he sits his fat body and curses his god, I think I'm human. He yells at me like I was human.

What the fuck are you looking at??

Who the hell do you think you are??

Sometimes he'll chase me around the room (it's a small place) and he tries to kick me. I flap my wings and jump around — to this side and that — to get away from him. When his foot connects, it hurts pretty bad, so I really try and get away, flapping around like a turkey pulled from the truck for the slaughter. He doesn't think about it when he does this, and he doesn't always do it. And afterwards, he's so apologetic that he cries and pulls out his hair. I come to him. He embraces me and tells me he's sorry. He holds me so tight, so tight sometimes, that I have no choice but to forgive him, and I do, but then I realize that I'm a duck, and forgiveness has no meaning. But feeling human, I try and make him happy. I look at him with my big eyes and I quack. He laughs at this, not a belly laugh or a guffaw, but a soft laugh. He tenders the rest of the morning with optimism. He says things like, "Today will be a good day!"

Then he gets on his hat, gathers together our stuff, the tape recorder, the sign, the can, the blanket, and we leave the apartment and get into the VW Bug. We drive to the plaza. All day long people pass and look at me and say those meaningless words as they try to pat me on the head like a dog. But I'm a duck. I waddle around. They put money in the can. I do my job.

SKY RATS

Two pigeons were dying. One was on its side, breathing heavy, some sort of thick, greenish ooze coming from its mouth, and the other one was still sitting up, flapping its wings, as if it could just fly off, but that one was dying too. A little boy holding the hand of his stupid-looking father pointed at the birds and asked his father what was happening, but daddy said he didn't know. The boy started crying. He said, "Help them." The father looked around the plaza, as if some superhero would come and save the day. He looked at me, and I shrugged my shoulders.

Other pigeons were dying too, a whole bunch of them under the tree that shaded most of the plaza. Some of the soon-to-be dead birds could still walk around, like drunkards, but others, in the more advanced stages of dying, could only fall on their sides, breathing slowly, heavily, deliberately, that goo oozing out of their beaks. One young pigeon, thin and with a long smooth neck, still had enough strength to fly off, but only for a few feet, and then he landed again, tried to fly again, until his young body caved in, and he landed with a thud on the stone. He tilted and fell to his side, breathed hard, and gave up his spirit.

People in the outdoor cafe were murmuring, "What could it be?" Some man in a red cap suggested it was the heat. This was the summer of that heat wave, the canicule that was so bad that old people died in the hell of their own non-air-conditioned flats. "It's the heat," Red Cap suggested. Others disagreed.

"These kinds of birds are survivors," I said to the father, who was standing next to me, looking dumbly at the birds, the boy's head buried in his chest.

"They don't just die like this," I said. "This is something else."

Some tourist was taking pictures of all the dead and dying birds. A teenage girl with a piercing in her lip covered her eyes in sadness. People asked each other and themselves in various languages what must have happened, why were all the birds dying.

The girl with the pierced lip looked up into the sky, as if she expected some dead birds would just fall down like a shower of frogs.

"Should we call someone?" some man with a briefcase asked the crowd.

"Who?" some woman replied.

"Let's call the police," the father said.

That's when I said something.

"The police? What for? It's not like some crime has been committed."

The crowd was listening to me.

"This is *super* natural. Maybe it's God's way of telling us something, something big that's about to happen. Maybe this is an omen. If you think about it, this is pretty amazing. Birds don't just die. Not this many."

At that statement a few people looked up into the sky. Others nodded their heads, as if they, too, had been thinking about God.

"The police can't do anything to help them," I said pushing my hand into my pants' pocket, pushing the small box of poison further down, so no one would be able to see the bulge in my pants.

VELOCITY OF MASS

F ather Flood rushed through life so fast that Sunday
Mass lasted 40 minutes, and the daily Mass — which
usually took about 30 minutes — rushed by in less
than 15. He was the oldest priest at Our Lady of Sorrow,
and he had been giving Mass for so long and knew it so
well that when the laic deacon held open the big, red holy
book during the Eucharist, Flood didn't read from it at all.
He had it all memorized, in Spanish, English, French, and
Latin. He said it so automatically that his mind wandered
to other things and his voice resonated throughout the
nave, mumbling words so fast that nobody could keep up.
The sound of his voice was heavy and thick, like a cello in
a wooden room, like the thud of clay falling on hardened
dirt. It resonated and vibrated in the dome on the ceiling,
which reached high up and was lined with slats of stained
glass. On the outside side of the glass, pigeons nested.

Morning and afternoon sun coming from the
windows in the dome was the only light, but when clouds
passed and the sanctuary grew dim, Father Flood did not
slow down. He didn't need light for speed.

Some parishioners preferred Father Flood over
the young priests. They took so long saying each word of
the prayers, like a wooden waterwheel, as if they meant to
slowly water their garden. They said their words as if they
meant them, and that caused the parishioners to think of
life. People didn't have to think standing among the flowing
sound of the old man's words, they could just submit to
the speed of his voice and let their worries run loose from

their minds, like children rushing from the house to play in a field. When the Mass was over, they rushed from the house of God into the city, feeling a sense of freedom and purpose they didn't have without his Mass. Father Flood became popular with busy, important people, who, upon entering the nave, would turn around and leave if it wasn't Father Flood presiding.

At first, the young priests ignored the fast Masses of Father Flood, but then something happened that increased their concern.

He began to mumble Mass in other languages, sometimes in Spanish, the language of the city, but other times in English or French or Latin, and sometimes all four tongues in the same prayer. The young priests got together and decided that there was nothing they could do, that Father Flood was already in his eighties or his nineties or maybe he was over a hundred, nobody knew for sure, but they knew that the most merciful thing to do was nothing. He had no desire to retire, and quite frankly, he couldn't give Mass much longer. He could barely walk. He hadn't ascended the spiral stairs to the bell tower in many years or walked around the neighborhood, which he used to love to do. He could barely see, needing glasses even to discern light coming through the open doors of the church.

They decided to allow him to conduct morning Mass but only morning Mass. He would no longer do Holy Days of Obligation. He would no longer listen to confessions.

But then it got worse.

He got confused about the time of day, and he showed up on the altar one evening in his Mass clothes. It was a Sunday, the busiest, most important service of the church, the bread and butter for the bills. Two young priests were giving the Mass, the youngest reading the gospel, slowly pronouncing Mark 4:22. Father Flood didn't notice. He raised his arms to heaven and began a second Mass. The young priest — so engrossed in the energy of his reading — didn't notice the old man until his voice started to echo his own, and then overtake it.

When he was a middle-aged priest, new to the city, new to the continent, he used to like to walk around Villa Freud, which was mostly high-rise apartment buildings with ground-level cafés and shops. Day and night people walked by on the sidewalks, buses passed, taxis wove in and out of traffic. A subway stop was a few blocks away. He liked to talk to people in the neighborhood, although at first he had to get used to their Spanish, different from his own. He began to like the city, and liked to think of it as the Manhattan of Latin America. He liked to browse the art section of the bookstores, looking at the great paintings, at statues and frescoes, at art photography. He liked to sit on park benches or talk to the girl who sold flowers from a booth in a small plaza, and although he never learned her name, over the years, he watched her become a young woman. Then one day, when she was in her mid twenties, the girl was gone, gone was the smell of wet roses, and the booth stood empty for weeks, until it was removed.

After 20 years in the city, he could think of no other place as home, and the times he had to travel abroad, he was eager to get back to the city he loved to walk. When he became a very old man, and his Masses started to go so fast, he was unable to walk as much. As he grew older still, he didn't enjoy his meals, and when the old woman who worked for the church came to his room with a steaming bowl of hominy and intestines, he would tell her he wasn't hungry. The young priests didn't visit him in his room, because he talked about the past, and he got chronological time confused. He would be telling of when he was a young priest in Rome, giving Mass in Latin, and mid-sentence, his story would take place 30 years later, when the military came with trucks and guns, how they collected young people they thought were a threat, including a few good nuns and some young priests like him, and he had to hide underneath the church, right under the skirt of the Virgin, a secret place under the altar.

The young priests ignored his senility. He would die soon, and they waited. And waited. And waited for a very long time. More years passed, and the young priests got old. They went on to other congregations, got promoted within the church, quit the cloth for romantic love or doubt or scandal or all three, but Father Flood remained. He gave thousands and thousands of Masses at such high speed that the church became popular with busy people from other neighborhoods. The older he got, the shorter the Masses became. You couldn't keep up even if you were following along in the missal. After a while, morning Mass lasted 10 minutes. His following became even bigger, because people who would otherwise not waste their time going to Mass *every* day could certainly spend 10 minutes in a Mass so fast that it was like a shot of whiskey.

This is when it happened.

Everyone one would talk about it for years. The Vatican would keep an extensive file on it, including eyewitness accounts and expert opinions, and maybe one day they would decide to make it an official miracle. It started one uneventful Wednesday morning when people knew Father Flood would be giving Mass. The aisles were full of business people and some were even standing by the doors. But six o'clock came by, and Father Flood had not come out. The laic deacon, an old man who assisted the Father in giving the Mass, was named Daniel, a retired psychologist who lived in Villa Freud. He stood on the altar waiting, wondering, looking at the parishioners and shrugging his shoulders. Father Flood had never been late before.

When he walked out seven minutes later, people could not believe what they saw. What little silver hair he had left was disheveled, and his eyes were baggy and red, as if he hadn't slept in weeks. His undershirt was wrinkled and stained, and he wore no pants, just a baggy pair of boxers. He looked almost dead, his cheeks sunken in, his eyes hollow. He was pale. He walked onto the altar like entering a room he had never seen. Daniel retrieved his robe, and put it over the priest's head. He straightened it out and whispered, "Can you do this today?" The priest didn't answer. He walked to the center of the altar and looked at the people, as if wondering who they were and why they were there.

Every Catholic knows that at the beginning of Mass, the priest leads parishioners into a prayer of forgiveness. Once forgiven, they can go into the ceremony pure. That was not how it happened that day. Father Flood raised his old hands to the dome and said, "The Lord be with you." The parishioners answered back, "And with your spirit," but the father went right into the Lord's Prayer, in multi-languages.

"Padre nuestro
qui est dans le ciel
santificado sea
your name."

Everybody knew that his Mass was very fast — the fastest Mass in the world — but they were confused as to why he went from the beginning right to the Lord's Prayer, which was supposed to be toward the end. They looked to each other, maybe hoping that Mass would only last five minutes. They obediently held each other's hands up in the air and recited the Lord's Prayer: "Danos hoy nuestro pan"...

But before they could reach the end, he suddenly began to utter words that came right after the readings, "This is the word of God."

The businessmen and -women, the housewives and active middle-class moms said, "Glory to you, Lord." They wondered, "Did they already take up the collection and we didn't notice?" But then Father Flood began to recite the words to the profession of faith, even though that didn't come at the right time either. The beginning was the middle was the end was the middle again. Father Flood went on and on and on and recited prayers over and over again in different order and in four languages. He held up the cup and repeated the words Jesus had spoken to the disciples, and then he put the cup down and began the Lord's Prayer again. He kept saying kneel and stand and sit and kneel again so that the parishioners moved up and down like frenzied sports fans. The new young priest across the nave giving confessions didn't understand what was going on, and he thought that maybe it was he himself who was losing track of linear time. He held onto his chair like someone on a bumpy ride. But the Mass went on.

And on. And on.

Some people left after the first 20 minutes. They shook their heads in disgust, touched their wallets — happy that they didn't give.

An hour passed.

Others people, however, stayed around, as if there was something powerful about the way Father Flood was feeding them, weaving this prayer with that. Two hours passed. Sentences went back and forth between English and Spanish and French and Latin, and the swirl of words — the twists and screws and incomprehensible incantations — enchanted the silence which suddenly filled the dome.

Father Flood was silent.

The nave was quiet.

The third hour passed.

Then he started again, in the middle or the end or the beginning. According to the Vatican files, one old woman who always wore a red scarf to Mass, who lived in the building across the street and went to services twice a day and three times on Sunday, believed that this was a sign from God. Even as she began to feel hungry and thirsty, she stayed, kneeling and sitting and standing, according to the words. It was during this time that she realized something about herself: she knew what the results of her tests would be, knew it was fatal, but she also knew that it was O.K., she was ready to die.

By midnight, not only were there still many parishioners left — as if being held in the church by a physical force — but curious passersby walking along the sidewalk outside nd hearing Mass going on so long and late felt themselves sucked in, and they peeked into the nave, and some of them stayed. Then the seasonal rains came to the city, falling so hard that trees grew out of cracks in the sidewalks and water rushed through the gutters. Homeless people, wet and without shelter, were happy to enter into the warm light of the open doors.

By three in the morning, the young priests gathered at the far end of the nave and watched the Mass go on and on, but they didn't stop it, because it was clear that people in the neighborhood thought there was something special going on. The church stayed full, and every time the collection baskets went around — every ten minutes or every two minutes or every hour — the redeemed reached deeply into their pockets and gave.

The next morning those who were used to coming to six o'clock Mass thought that they were late, because when they walked in, the prayers had already started. They sat and looked around, confused, but after a while the mixture of the prayers and the non-linear incantations flowing from Father Flood lulled them into a trance, like a fragrance from a bottle. People prayed like they had had never prayed before. And even though this was not a charismatic church — but a very conservative Catholic congregation — some began to speak in tongues. They raised their hands to the Lord and they praised him in languages they themselves didn't understand. People danced. Others prophesied, yelled out loud what God was saying to them. The voices that filled the church, weaving around the chord of Father Flood's voice — hundreds and hundreds and thousands and millions of voices — were mixing and swirling so fast that the energy almost became Mass and brushed against the doors and the windows, and the pigeons on the dome flew off. People were cured. The blind could see. The young priests couldn't get through to the cardinal, because every time they tried, somehow the phone connection went bad.

In the next few days, so many people had gone in and out of that church, any time of night or day, that it became a pilgrimage, a holy destination not only for Catholics (who would wait all day in line just to see the image of the Virgin in a pizza), but for people everywhere. According to the Vatican files, some Mennonites came from thousands of miles away, just to bask in the spirit, and there were Jews, too, mostly Kabbalists, and Sufi Muslims, and Buddhists.

News cameras parked outside, documentaries were planned, magazines sent reporters and photographers.

But Father Flood was old. Other than the host, he hadn't eaten, and other than the wine mixed with water, he hadn't drank. He began to get weak, and he began to slow down.

He enunciated every word.

As he slowly spoke, he remembered things.

He saw his father killing a chicken. Saw his sister's ankle as she stepped onto a city tram. Saw Rome at night, a well-lit café, a drunk man and woman walking out, leaning on each other and laughing. He saw a pool of water in the cup of his hands, rising to meet his own reflection. He saw the girl who had sold flowers, wrapping a bunch of unsmelled roses in white paper. He saw the snowy mountains that loom outside of his home village, and from afar they looked like his own face.

And during that time, when things were quite slow, almost quiet, when his voice spoke only one word at a time, people wept. They thought of their lives, and they wept.

Father Flood became so weak that the new young priests had to hold him up, one on each side, so that the old man could continue to raise his arms and weep the words of Mass, like Moses on the mountaintop, looking across the river, looking down on a promise he would never touch.

THE CITY IN WHICH HE IMAGINED

"J'espère que les chiens ne aboieront pas cette nuit.
Je crois toujours que c'est le mien."
L'Etranger

As he walked into the underground subway station, he imagined he heard a doorbell ring, *ding dong ding dong*, but he ignored it, because it couldn't have been an actual doorbell, not underneath the ground in Buenos Aires, not competing with the thundering roar of metal on the tracks. Still, he heard a doorbell in his imagination, *ding dong ding dong*, like what one would hear back home.

He imagined that one of the maintenance workers in the subway station wanted to make his janitor's closet seem like home, since he probably had to spend so much time away from his own. He always like passing janitor's closets and looking in, seeing the radio on a shelf whispering the ballgame, seeing framed pictures of the janitor's kids on an upside-down crate set up like a table. Maybe this janitor put a doormat in front of the threshold, and it said "Hogar dulce hogar", and maybe he rigged a doorbell so other janitors, visiting him, could ring as if dropping by his home. Maybe the janitor had hung a calendar on the wall of his closet, held with tape, because he liked the image, which was a colorful painting of *San Gil*, the Gaucho Saint of Argentina. He had long, beautiful hair, like a pretty woman, and the bushy mustache of a man. The janitor he imagined was fat and hairy, and he imagined seeing him sitting in his janitor's closet on an upside down bucket, eating his dinner, radio announcing the La Boca game.

His logic wouldn't allow his imagination to go any further with the janitor's closet scenario. Doorbells in Buenos Aires were different. Everything in Buenos Aires was different. Water drained down the sink in the opposite direction, keys were skeletons, like those used by his ancestors. The fat, hairy janitor would be more likely to hang a bell with a string, and people could stand before his door and ring it. There had to be another explanation as to why he was hearing a doorbell. Suddenly a thought occurred to him: He could be hearing an *actual* doorbell, not coming from the sound waves vibrating around in the underground, but sound coming from a memory, not personal memory, but a communal memory. Maybe the doorbell was a sound from another time and space. He imagined a door opening in the walls of the underground station, a brick wall, a breach large enough for him to see into the light of another reality.

He liked to imagine other realities. Sometimes at night in Buenos Aires, as he tried to sleep, the city moaned beyond his open balcony, and he thought it sounded like a thousand voices of the dead calling from the other world. Every now and then one voice rose out of the roar — a man's scream, a woman's groan — and then it would sink back into the water of voices. The sheer white curtains in the balcony doors rippled in the breeze, and he heard the squeaky wheels of the poor pass below his window. At these times, when he wanted to sleep, he closed his eyes and tried. Sometimes, as happens to us all, he unwittingly saw images in his inner eye. Maybe he would see a seemingly random place back home, an intersection of strip malls, a tree-lined path he took to class as a university student, a food stand on Venice Beach where a black man in a white robe holds a sign that says, "Repent. The end is near."

Sometimes he would get images of a place he had never seen, perhaps a conglomerate of images from places in his psyche coming out together to create something new in his imagination. The place in his mind's eye might look familiar, maybe a parking lot under streetlamps; a stone square with a hole in it, where a tree used to be; a brick wall with a crack; an empty field with a single tree; a gate in an alley. He knew this happened to everyone, images pass before people's eyes, and like most people he assumed that the images were random. They meant nothing. But he was a computer systems manager, responsible for putting networks together, connecting a world of things, and he began to imagine that the universe worked the same way. All things were connected, especially humans, who, in his imagination, were like PCs. One unit should be able to access the entire network and influence the flow of information.

He began to pretend on those sleepless nights that what he was seeing in his mind's eye was not random, but rather *he*, as a unit or soul, was being connected to another part of the network, another soul, which came from that particular place in his imagination on that particular night as he lay in bed trying to sleep. He pretended it was like a vision, some reason beyond himself, some call for help from some other PC in the network. He would see the place so clearly in his mind's eye, so clearly, as if he were watching a video downstream on his computer.

As he waited for the next subway train, the doorbell still ringing in his mind's ear, he imagined that on those sleepless nights when he saw places in his inner eye, something was about to happen at that particular spot, maybe something bad. Maybe at the food stand on Venice Beach a murder was about to happen, or on that tree-lined path at the university a rapist hid in the shadows of the pine trees. Maybe for some reason God (or the system of connections) was allowing him to see through other units. Nothing was random. For centuries people have searched for the meaning of their dreams, and through dreams they have discovered profound truths, as if dreams were letters from God. Why couldn't the non-sleeping Dreams, those quick images that involuntarily come to our minds as we try to sleep, also have meaning? Like memos from God?

The other night, before he was asleep, he had seen a gas station near the house where he grew up in West L.A. It was a Chevron on the intersection of Lincoln and Washington. He saw the place so clearly in his mind as he lay in bed thousands of miles away. He got hot, and he threw the sweaty sheets off his body like an angry lover. Maybe he was seeing that Chevron for a reason. Maybe it was a warning that something was about to happen there, and he was supposed to do something, but he was halfway around the world. He was impotent to help. He couldn't pick up the phone and call the LAPD and say, "I'm calling from Buenos Aires. . . No, not Brazil. It's in Argentina. . . Yes, and uh, I think something might be about to happen on Washington Blvd. I'm not sure what it will be, but could you send a squad car over there to check it out?"

Maybe this doorbell he heard ringing in his mind while underground waiting for the next subway was a real doorbell, but in another place. It sounded real, but it was impossible to be coming from where he stood. It sounded so familiar. He could even picture the house within which the bell sounded. He could picture a tree-lined street, sidewalks smooth and clean.

The next train would still be some minutes in arriving. He sat on a bench. He closed his eyes and tried to imagine the breach in the fabric of space so he could see inside to that other place. He pictured the doorbell's house from the curb. The house appeared to be in Culver City, one of those tree-lined streets with well-kept homes.

He saw a brick house. There was a dim porch light on, because it was night. There was a wooden bench on the porch, empty but for a basket of walnuts, probably picked from the giant walnut tree out front, which darkened the yard, hid the moon, so he saw no moon. Some of the branches hung so low to the ground that the yard couldn't be seen from the street. He saw through the branches, because in his imagination, he was going up the walkway to the front door. He smelled the trees. He smelled the honeysuckle. Something was about to happen to the units who lived in that house, and he needed to warn them. Was there a killer underneath the walnut tree?

Then a horrible thought occurred to him.

He opened his eyes. People were gathering on the platform, waiting for the next train. The janitor, on the other side of the tracks, was pulling garbage bags from the trashcans.

He knew that if he closed his eyes again, he would go right back to the other place.

What if the network he was accessing wasn't the one in which he lived? What if it was an entirely different system, an entirely different universe? What if the house in his imagination was *his* house? What if it was the house he never had? What if he shared it with the wife he never married (for some reason he understood her name was Claire) and with kids he never fathered, a boy and a girl, precocious kids? This is how his life would have been had he made different choices, and now, something was about to happen to them. He closed his eyes again, entered that other place. He wanted to travel to the other network and help.

The front window of the house was large and wide, a bay window. It framed the living room. Inside was oak and leather furniture, shadow and light. He imagined himself walking up the sidewalk, to the front door. He could see his vague reflection in the window, a hooded figure, a dark shadow, a blur. He saw a flash of the white of his eyes. But what was he doing there?

Why was he allowed to slip through that breach into this other place, this other world, reversed from his own, maybe a place from where someone imagined him? Maybe his doppelganger was somewhere inside the house as the doorbell was ringing, and for no reason, he was hearing the clanking rails of an underground subway train in Buenos Aires.

But no. He knew that no one was home but Claire. He saw himself standing on the porch, and he realized that it was himself who was ringing the doorbell.

He saw a light go on. It spread onto the wooden floors of the living room, and he saw a blue silhouette of a woman. She held a leather-bound book. She put it face down on a small table with a brass lamp. "Coming," she said, in a voice that broke his heart, because it was Claire's voice.

He wanted to warn her not to answer. There was danger, something bad, and Claire was alone. The husband (his doppelganger) was gone, as were the two kids. The dog was there, and he was barking, but from the sound of it you knew he was a tiny dog, probably a little white thing with a red ribbon around his delicate neck. Such a small dog couldn't have been for protection, couldn't have scared off anyone.

Don't answer the door, he wanted to yell to Claire, but her footsteps got closer and closer. He rang the bell over and over again, *ding dong, ding dong*, wanting her to hear him, *Please don't answer that door*. He heard her body on the other side. Felt the warmth of her body on the other side. He heard her undo the chain — she didn't even look through the peephole — and he heard the door handle jiggle and he saw it slowly turn. *No*, he wanted to say, *it's a killer. You're in danger*, but the door opened.

In a roar of metallic noise and wind, the subway train came shooting from the tunnel. It stopped on the tracks and the doors slid open. A bunch of people got out, and they walked to the stairs that led up from the underground. The people waiting on the platform packed into the train and took their seats.

But he stayed seated on the bench. He heard the warning buzzer that the subway doors were about to close. He heard the doors close. He put his elbows on his knees, put his face in his hands, and he wept. "I'm sorry, Claire," he cried. "I fucked up. I'm sorry."

The doorbell rang, more and more, faster and faster, a rapid succession of rings. He didn't notice the three boys coming up behind him. He was not fully aware of what was happening to him as they dragged him away from the lights and into the dark tunnel. He saw the gleam of a blade, felt a blow on the side of his head, but mostly he heard the doorbell, louder and louder, like a warning, *Ding dong! DING DONG!*

DA DA DO

Nick Nick was Nick Nick, not Nick, not Nicolas, but Nick Nick. No one knows why his mother called him that. She had him when she was 13 years old, and maybe she had her reasons, maybe she was delirious, but that's what it says on his birth certificate, Nick Nick Gomez. Sometimes he told people his name was just Nick, but somehow they would see his name in writing and they'd say something like, "They made a mistake!" or: "Look, a typo!" and Nick thought to himself, that's me, "A typo." Maybe that was why his 13-year-old mother held him for a few months and then disappeared, leaving Nick Nick with his young grandmother (she was 30 when her daughter left) in a brick house near the river. is uncle was a few years later, and they shared a bedroom. The young uncle snored so loud that Nick Nick couldn't hear the river.

The brick house was isolated from the rest of town, but there was a trail through the trees that led to a wooden bridge across the river, which Nick Nick and his uncle took to school when they were kids. Years later, when he was an old man, Nick Nick used to walk along that path, and his caretaker (provided by the county) would go find him to call him for supper. She would see old Nick Nick sitting on a rock talking to the water, telling it his secrets.

So Nick Nick lived in this house all his life, leaving town only once, for 10 years, the time he went off to get his college degrees, which culminated with a PhD from Harvard Divinity School. He had always been a great student, but Harvard wasn't easy to get into. His grades and test scores got him in, and being a poor, orphaned Chicano, he got scholarships. "My 13-year-old mother was a drug addict and a prostitute," he wrote on his personal statement. He imagined that detail. Yes, she was an addict, but there's no evidence that she was ever a prostitute. Nick Nick wrote that being a Chicano child of a 13-year-old drug addict and prostitute was torture. His father, he wrote, was any combination of possibilities drawn from all the men in town, which at the time of his birth had a population of 22,000. Nick Nick imagined that maybe he had a mixture of fathers, one part sperm from one man, one from another, sperm from this one, sperm from that, sperm from the butcher, sperm from the baker, etc. He imagined that he most resembled not one, but four or five men, maybe six men. He liked the number six (when he was a kid, the written number reminded him of a pregnant woman sitting on her butt) so he liked to imagine he had six fathers. He even named them: Stanley, Horace, Richard, Malcolm, Emiliano, Elijah, Pepe, and Hogan. About his six fathers: He didn't put this in his personal statement for grad school, but he thought of it.

He got a full ride and, quite frankly, Nick Nick was a genius. He graduated high school when he was 11 years old, taught himself calculus at 13, built a computer the summer of his fourteenth year, and by 16 years old, he had read so many books, everything from seven volumes of Swedenborg to the physicist Schrödinger's *What is Life,* that he couldn't read a book or see a movie without applying all he had learned about reality to narrative imagery, metaphor, and matter. He found most artistic and scholarly perceptions to be superficial. He needed to be around minds that challenged him. He started playing Scrabble with his uncle and grandmother, but they were inane. He'd put simple words down like "pith" or "lam" and they would challenge him. His uncle, who had a big bottom lip and doubled his words, would say, "That-that ain't a word-word."

"How would you know?" he asked.

"Can't-can't fool me, Nick Nick-Nick Nick (he actually only said "Nick Nick" but with his tendency to double words it came out Nick Nick-Nick Nick).

At sixteen Nick Nick was so bored with life that adult ennui kicked in. The once-magical walk through the forest — where even the trees would speak with him — suddenly became drab and gray. Rocks were rocks and trees were trees and the river was only a river. That was when he applied as an undergraduate to Berkeley, and he got a full ride, majoring in physics, philosophy, and linguistics. He graduated the top of his class. They asked him to make a speech at the graduation ceremony, but he didn't want to. He hated crowds and special events. When his grandmother and his stupid uncle came into Berkeley for his graduation, he suggested that instead of the ceremony, they should take the BART train to San Francisco and eat dim sum in Chinatown. "What's-what's Dim-Dim Sum-Sum?" asked his uncle.

After Berkeley, this Chicano genius was fought over by graduate programs at Yale, Harvard, Berkeley, and Fresno State. He chose Harvard, because he figured there he might find the greatest minds to challenge him. He breezed through and got bored with most of his classes. He only liked to research and write papers. He was offered a publication contract for his dissertation (*The Physics of Torah*), wherein he argued that the greatest emanation of G-d, which is love, could be arrived at by converting — with a simple mathematical equation — the metaphorical landscape of Genesis and Exodus into quantum theory, which is imageless (without metaphor) and therefore closer to the energy that gives form to matter. One could evoke through mathematics a true unification with the divine, he argued.

He was offered countless jobs and fellowships, but his uncle, his stupid uncle had contacted some weird disease that kept him bedridden. His grandmother still worked full-time at the bakery, so he decided that if he believed anything he had ever read and studied, and if Mercy was one of the cabalistic emanations on the Tree of Life, he'd better take care of his uncle. Besides, he had no desire to teach. He hated people. So he came back to town, which now had a population of about 44,000. He was 22, a Harvard Ph.D with a book.

He liked being at home, because he would simply wait for the mailman to come to the brick house with a new box of books, and he would read, he would take walks along the river, sit on his rock and talk to the water. He sometimes walked across the bridge, over the river, and stood there in the middle. He would contemplate a tree, a squirrel, the veins in his hand. He liked life, especially since he didn't have to share it with anyone or hear their inane opinions. Still, he hated taking care of his stupid, invalid uncle. The brick house was two bedrooms, but Nick Nick didn't sleep anymore in his uncle's room, because the illness caused is uncle to belch and fart and vomit, so the smell in there was horrible. Plus, all the uncle liked to do in his lucid moments was watch porn. He had piles of X-rated videos falling out of the closet like multi-colored treasure, hardcore porn that disturbed Nick Nick to see.

He slept on the couch, but he woke up each morning with a crick in his neck, and he'd be grumpy all day and would be passive-aggressively cruel to his uncle. One day his grandma said, "Nick Nick, why don't you sleep with me in my bed? It's big enough." So he did, for the next several years, until his uncle died and he had the room cleaned and sprayed, and he moved in there. "I'm going to miss you," his grandmother said, kissing him on the forehead, as if he were a little boy going off to summer camp.

But the most important moment of his life happened to Nick Nick when he was 99 years old. He was going to die that day, but of course, he thought it was just another day. He went into town, which was no longer a town but a city of 122,000 people, and he bought some groceries to make sandwiches. The clerk at the store was a young woman with bored eyes and a nametag that said "Rose." She was listening to a radio, some rock music. She put the items in his bag, bologna, white bread, mustard, pickles. Then she closed the bag and smiled at him. "I bet I know what you're having for lunch," she said.

Then he started his walk back home, across the bridge over the new freeway, across the bridge over the river. This day was his last, the end of his life. This was long after his 13-year-old mother came back at 45 years old and looked like a crack junkie, asking Nick Nick for a little something, anything; and this was long after his uncle died in his sleep, staying there for a week surrounded by pizza boxes, porn, and tiny fists of Kleenex stained yellow with dried semen; long after his grandmother quit her job at the bakery, spent the last ten years of her life watching TV and bad-mouthing the government; long after his book, *The Physics of Torah*, went into its ninth printing and was called by a religious studies journal one of the most important books of the century; this was long after Nick Nick had fallen in love with a girl twenty years younger than him, her 22, he 44, when he saw her sitting on his rock, telling the river her troubles. This day of his death was long after their short marriage and her drowning in the river at the age of 32.

This is what the story is about.

He was 99. When he got back from the grocery store, he entered the brick house. It was so silent he could hear the cars on the new freeway. He thought about Rose, the cashier at the store, and he suddenly felt a desire to hear some contemporary music, but he didn't know of any, just things like Bach and Berlioz. But for some reason, he craved rock and roll. He turned on the radio, which was set to the last station his grandmother had listened to before she died, some Spanish-language AM station that played Banda and Mariachi. He played with the dial and he came to 91.2 FM. Some young, cool-sounding deejay said, "Next up: an old one from back in the days: The *The*."

The song went like this:
Da da do
Dabee doobee dabee do.
Da da do
Dabee doobee dabee do.
And then, much to Nick Nick's amazement, the next words after *da da do* were,
Nick Nick
Nick Nick
Nick Nick
Nick
It was as if The *The* was singing to him, saying his name over and over.

At that moment, he suddenly felt that everything in the universe, everything in that small brick house, everything in the town, everything everywhere was connected to everything else. He had known this all his life — that's what his book was about — but hearing the song by The *The* made him realize that he had never really believed it, not really, but that *Da da do*, that rock and roll song written by someone who didn't even know him spoke to him on a deeper level than any book, any religion, any experience. Nick Nick suddenly felt himself dissolve (he was dying, but didn't know it), as if the atoms that made up his flesh separated and became part of everything else, all other atoms. He felt himself becoming part of the quantum field, swimming like a particle in the waves of the electro-magnetic energy that came from the radio, where the young clerk at the grocery store listens to rock, part of the sound waves from the river, the freeway, the creaks of the wooden floors in the brick house, part of the quarks and neutrinos that made up and passed through the table and chairs where they had once played Scrabble, the bed where his uncle used to sleep –Nick Nick was pizza boxes, phlegm and vomit, and it was beautiful. He had such a great affection, a great love for everything, even the freeway — where all day and night, all around the ticks of the clock, cars moved both ways, from the past into the future. This is a story about the day Nick Nick was born.

DANIEL 13

Night and day among the tombs and in the hills
he would cry out and cut himself with stones.

Mark 5:5

ONE

Everyday the two old men saw the young woman working in her husband's orchard. Some mornings they watched her climb a ladder to the top of a tree, feel the oranges, sniff them, and sometimes, they saw her claw them open and taste the juices. Her husband owned miles and miles of fruit trees, oranges, lemons, and grapefruits, one of the richest men in the San Joaquin Valley. When he had married Susana, everyone was shocked that a rich rancher, 30 years older, a man with no heirs and much wealth and land, would marry the daughter of one of his farm workers, a man named Calderón. Her father was a religious man from Michoacán, always giving to the church, making the sign of the cross, praying to the Virgin, and he raised Susana to fear God. She was quite beautiful, and at 22 years old, upon marrying the old white man, she became one off the richest women in the valley. Her sudden position, a Latina with power, a Chicana with money, thrust her into many social spotlights. She became a community leader, a role model for the farmworker children, and she took her responsibility seriously, believing that the Lord had blessed her, and she needed to do the most good she could for others. She organized charities for immigrant children, helped organize literacy programs, and she continued to take classes at the college, where she joined the Chicano/a student organization. She loved every one of the workers on her land, and they loved her, and worked harder because of her.

Each morning she would get up before dawn and walk by herself through the orchards, sometimes the morning fog shrouding her like a veil. She stood among the trees and imagined she could hear God speak through the wind, through the color of fruit, and the way the plump oranges, ready to eat, fell from the stems into her hands. The first year of her marriage, the trees produced more fruit than ever before, and the oranges were the sweetest in the land.

In the spring, she walked among the blossoms, and the two old men, one who owned the grape fields across the street, watched her.

One didn't know the other felt the same way about her, but they became so obsessed with her lithe figure in the orchards that they couldn't sleep at night for thinking of her. They turned around in bed and saw their own ugly wives, and they began to believe that they had legitimate reasons for not loving them anymore. Love fades, they told themselves. People change. They convinced themselves that they were in a loveless marriage, that their wives didn't love them either. They couldn't stop thinking of the pretty young woman walking barefooted through the orchards in a white dress moist with morning air.

The old men thought of her so much that they weren't able to get any work done, and they began to fail at everything. They were rich ranchers with assured livelihoods, but they began to lose money on a poor crop. In those brief moments of the day when they closed their eyes, sitting in their vehicles at a traffic light, sitting at a desk, they dreamed of her, imagined seeing her, and these images became sexually vivid. They knew that she would never fall in love with them, so in their hearts they made her a slut. She was a tease. She wanted them.

One morning, they were having coffee in the kitchen of one their homes, across the street from Susana's orchard. They looked out the window and saw her disappear into the fields, among trees and fog, a red ribbon in her hair. The air, wet with mist, made them imagine that she could take off her clothes and dance like a nymph among the trees. They wanted to spy on her, but they didn't know the other felt the same way about her, so they said goodbye, pretending that they had business to get to. They each walked into the foggy rows of fruit trees. It was cold, and in all directions they could only see as far as three rows of tree trunks. They heard occasional rustlings of small animals, some leaves slightly shaking, but all else was quiet. They listened for the one they wanted, imagined her walking barefoot, maybe dancing, her young figure twirling around, her hips showing through the white gown. Suddenly, they heard someone, footsteps, from beyond the trees. They stopped to listen.

At the exact same time as each other, they moved up a few paces. They were sure they had heard someone move up a few paces. They hoped to peek at her from behind a tree, hoped to see her climbing up and down a ladder, sliding up and down, all the way to the tops of the trees, her white gown glowing, all the way down to earth, her hands full with fat, ripe fruit. They slowly leaned their heads around a thick trunk, but what they saw was the face of the other.

"What are you doing here?" one old man asked.

They admitted to each other their lust for Susana.

Suddenly, they heard her voice humming a siren's song. It was too foggy to see her body in the trees, but the voice seemed to be moving away from the two old men, and it felt to them as if their hearts were being yanked out. One told the other he had seen the husband leave, that there was no one home, so they decided to follow her.

They saw her enter the house, her ankle the last thing they saw before the screen door shut. They hid in some bushes, near the windows of her bedroom, and they watched her, framed like a painting, white bedspread, white walls, brass-framed mirror. She stood there, humming a song and letting the dress slip from her body. She stepped out of her underwear. She walked out of her bedroom and down the hallway. The old men rushed to another window and saw her going into the bathroom. She stood before the basin and looked in the mirror, which reflected the upper half of her body. She raised her arms and put her hair in a bun. Her nipples were the color of chocolate.

The two old men each swallowed a pill of Viagra. They burst their way into her house and rushed into the bathroom.

She looked out of the shower curtains. They were known to her, because they were ranchers, leaders of the church, and they often met with her husband and other ranchers about water issues and weather.

"Have sex with us," one said.

"Are you crazy?" she said, and she yelled for help, but the men dragged her from the shower, down the hall, and into her bedroom. They pressed her wet, slippery body against the carpet, one holding down her shoulders, the other her hips.

"Don't make this hard," said one old man.

"We'll tell your husband we found you with some young guy," said the other. "Some young Pedro working in the fields. He'll believe us. Everyone will."

When one old man's shoulder was close enough to her mouth, Susana took a bite. The old man screamed and curled up in pain. She kicked the other man in the mouth with her heel, and when she stood and he fell, she kicked him again in the head. She grabbed a robe, ran out of the house with her cell phone, and she called for help.

At first, newspapers called it an attempted rape, but the old men asserted their power, and then some papers reported another version. Some suggested Susana had many young lovers, some said she had sex with workers, right in the fields. The headlines quit referring to the case as an attempted rape and called it a "Sex Scandal." The old men hired many false witnesses, men they paid to say that Susana had slept with them. That was why she disappeared each morning from her husband's bed, they said, to meet with her lovers in the orchards.

Some people reminded other people that she was a farmworker's daughter, a Mexican girl, and they suggested that values for those people were different. The fact that she was so much younger than her rich husband must mean she was up to something. Someone so young and beautiful — such a hot blooded Latina — how could she *not* have lovers?

One newspaper printed a picture of her wearing a strapless gown, laughing in the presence of some young, handsome man. The headline said, *The Private Life of An Heiress*. They didn't mention that the picture was taken at a literacy fundraiser, and she was standing next to her husband, who had been cropped out of the photo. They suggested that she had been planning to take her poor, naïve husband for all she could, and then to dump him, or worse, cut his throat, stab him multiple times, bury him in the fields.

The husband filed for divorce, and he commanded his lawyers to make sure she got nothing.

TWO

His name was Daniel. He was a cholo, a hardcore gangbanger, but one day something happened to him when he was walking around a Wal-Mart. He was high on PCP, Angel Dust, when suddenly his vision began to blur. Everything became formless, everything become muted colors, like a colorized black-and-white classic movie, and then all visible matter seemed to fade. Everything became particles floating in the air, which swirled around him like electrons, lights shooting up into heaven and back down into Wal-Mart. He felt invincible, like a terrible angel, like no object of matter could bump against him if he didn't will it. He could put his fist through concrete. Suddenly, his vision became clear and he saw, down an aisle of T-shirts hanging on glimmering silver racks, two guys from another gang, some 14ers, Norteños. It was like gift from heaven, because he felt like kicking some ass, it was as if he could make the universe provide what he wanted. He walked over to them and started on them, instantly pounding them to the ground. It was a brutal beating, and Daniel walked out of there that night with red on his hands, all the way to his wrists, as if he had been washing in a basin of blood.

He grew up in a small town surrounded by grape fields: Fowler, California. The children of the people who worked the fields went to the same school as the children of the ranchers who owned the fields: Fowler High. It enraged him the way they treated the Mexican kids, many who were in town only for the picking season and had no one to speak for them, so he figured he would give those people something to hate about Chicanos. He became a Sureño, a gang member. Teachers hated him, cops hated him, adults hated him, and their hatred made him angrier. By the time he was 16 he had swallowed so much rage that it began to burst from each vein, each muscle, each movement of his fingers. When someone called his name, they could see rage in the slow turn of his head, even someone at whom he would shoot a smile. Every word that came from his mouth was like an electric charge, so when he spoke, people shut up and listened. He tattooed the number of his gang on his neck, a giant 13. Even his own gang thought he was crazy, because this guy would walk into the midway at the Fresno County Fair with his tattooed 13 shining on his neck, looking at anyone who dared to look. He had gotten into so many fights that the knife scars were like an unfinished oil painting on his upper body.

Daniel loved that moment of clarity he had experienced on Angel Dust, when he had seen the veil rip open, and he wanted the feeling to last. He wanted to see like that everywhere he went, so he began to imagine energy vibrating in all things, trees, cars, dogs on chains, he imagined that the real world, the one we see and touch, was only the surface. Life was a superficial reality, the *real* reality was that which pulsed beyond the fabric of space. At this time in his life, he had no words for what he felt, for what he knew, because he was still an inarticulate boy of nineteen years, but he felt it, he felt there was something else, something missing. One day he got a tattoo of la virgen de Guadalupe on his back, a great big colorful canvas. He thought that she would protect him, maybe give him more of those moments of clarity. Then one night, drunk, high on Dust, he was walking by a church while the service was still going on. He could hear the singing. An evil feeling entered into him, and he got the idea — an image really — of walking into those lights and songs and all would stop and people would whisper to each other who he must be. He saw himself pulling people from the pews and beating them. He went inside.

The church was one of those Christian ministries that targeted people like him, gang members, drug addicts, and when he walked in nothing stopped. The singing was wild (WHAT A MIGHTY GOD WE SERVE!), people dancing, jumping up and down. One lady with a red scarf ran around the sanctuary, around and around, yelling something unintelligible. Some tough cholo guy was jumping up and down, some gang veterans had tears streaming from their eyes, their hands reaching to the light, as if they knew, they knew, there was something pulsing on the other side. People in the church moved over on the pews to give Daniel room.

He never left. All that rage, all that undeveloped energy that pulsed under his muscles and skin now went into his zealousness for God. He became a warrior for Christ, and, after a few months, the pastor of the church began to give Daniel more and more responsibilities. He led a Bible study for young people, he handed out tracks to gang members, the pastor trusted him so much that he gave him the keys to the church, office and all, and when someone needed something, they would call Daniel.

He started to take classes at the community college, he got a job, and he lived for God, but many people still thought he was a gang member. The sheriffs always stopped him to check him out, or they drove by him slowly, watching him with evil glares. Security followed him around department stores and malls, but instead of allowing this to turn into rage, he fed that energy into his love for them. He felt sorry for them, that they could not see beyond the veil, or even imagine it.

One night as he was walking along a rural road, sheriffs pulled him over, just to hassle him, but his eyes were filled with such love and his words flowed so freely that before they parted ways, they were on their knees in front of Daniel, in the dark grape fields, the silhouette of Daniel praying for them, his hands on their heads, looking up into the sky, shining with stars and planets.

Daniel first heard about the sex scandal after a service. People were talking about it on the steps of the church. "Women like that are dangerous," said one man. Daniel, having ministered to so many Latinos, so many Mexicanos, so many poor people of the fields, had heard that the workers loved Susana. She was a young Mexican woman, the daughter of a decent man. He was shocked to hear that people of his own church, many of them Latinos, some of them field workers, believed that she was guilty. They said things like, "I guess the old man couldn't give her what she wanted."

Daniel suddenly became enraged. He yelled, "How could you judge this woman? There has been no trial, no jury, yet you believe her guilt? Why?"

One afternoon he went into the office of the pastor and told him they should do something about it, it was an injustice, she was a godly Catholic, good to the workers, and surely it was prejudice that turned the people against her. "Because she's a Mexicana," he said, "they treat her this way. The Bible tells us to defend the immigrant."

The pastor rolled his eyes and walked over to Daniel.

He put his hand on his shoulder and said, "Daniel, I know the Bible. I mean I know it pretty well. You're not seeing the big picture. Catholics are different from us. Most of them aren't even saved. They pray to the Virgin Mary, who was a woman, just a woman. They pray to *her.*"

Daniel thought of the Virgin tattooed on his back.

"Besides, this issue is not about race. Forgot about this. We got God's work to do."

But Daniel was jealous for his people, to him that was God's work, to defend his people, the immigrants, the oppressed, and it seemed like a sign from heaven when a couple of parishioners who had heard him defend Susana on the church steps came to him. They were workers on her ranch. One foggy morning, they told him, they had been working around the house, doing some raking and cleaning, when they saw the two old men watching her from the window, like nasty children. They saw the old men go into the back door of the house, and a minute later they heard her scream. They wanted to call the police, but they had no telephone, and they had no papers either, and they were afraid.

They saw Susana run out of the house, screaming and crying. She didn't see them. They didn't have time to think of what to do when suddenly the two old men ran out of the house and fled in opposite directions.

Daniel thought and prayed and meditated and took long walks though the fields and orchards when the idea came to him. He knew what had happened. He knew he had to do something, or the old men would get away with it. He needed to get each of the old men alone, thinking they would be meeting with Susana. He created and executed a plan to convince each of the old men separately, through letters and emails, that she wanted to

DANIEL 13

ask them to forgive her, but she told each one to keep it a secret from the other.

The old men, fat with arrogance and stupidity, reading the letters, believed it to be true. They agreed to meet her one night, and each of them chose the place themselves, the same place, the field of their fantasies, the fruit orchards of Susana's husband. They got ready for the big night. They put on cologne, they took an extra dose of Viagra, and each of them was thinking more or less the same thing: they wanted to have sex with her. One old man, thinking she should be punished, thought he would do it with her once, maybe twice, and then he would dump her, laugh at her as she sank back into poverty. The other old man really thought that he loved her, really pictured Susana as his wife, walking around the house in a thong, doing yoga naked on the floor of his living room, serving him dinner in a teddy.

The old men entered the darkness of the trees. The fog was knee-high, and the moon was shining down and making things blue and silver like a night scene from a play. They saw far away into the fields that Susana had lit red candles, a circle of them, like a lover's bed waiting for them. They walked closer and closer, seeing the candlelight shine on a silver ladder leaning against a tree, on top of which the oranges shone in the moonlight. Daniel, standing in the dark, waited for them to walk into the light of justice.

203

THE TREE THAT WOULDN'T
LEAVE SARA ALONE
a children's fable (maybe)

Have you ever seen a tree at night, maybe as you're looking out a window onto a dark field, and it looks like a giant skeleton? Or maybe you're in the backseat of a car or you're in a train, and you're moving fast through a sleepy neighborhood, and you see new peach trees in the backyards and they look like children playing in the moonlight? This happens to us all the time, because trees have spirits, just like you and me. That's what you're seeing.

This is a story about a tree with a lot of spirit, so much that it fell in love, so I guess you could say this is a love story. This tree was about a hundred and fifty years old, and it was an oak tree. It was strong and firm, and the earth liked the tree, because its roots tickled the earth's belly.

Trees don't have human names, they are not Sandy, Ricky and Danny or Pedro or Maya and Steven, because those who gave them human names and the children of those who gave them human names usually die before the tree.

Our oak tree didn't have a human name, but to make the telling of this story easy, we'll call him Hubert. This tree, the big oak tree who fell in love, was the only oak tree left in an open field on the edge of the city. The city was getting bigger and full of more and more people, spreading out, getting closer and closer to the field, but Hubert had been there when the city was young and far away, and the field was an orchard of fig trees, now dead. Before that, he remembered it was a field of poppies, and even before that, he had a few infant memories of when the field was a gathering of oak trees like him, healthy and strong, trees spreading as far as the river, which was dried up now.

When this story takes place, the city was expanding. They destroyed the fields and orchards and turned them into subdivisions and shopping centers. The entire field was about to be leveled flat to become a development of new homes with three-car garages. Hubert had no choice but to resign himself to the fact of a future among people, and he hoped, at least, to be in the backyard of humans who had kids.

On one edge of Hubert's field was a freeway — always busy with cars — and on the other side of that were a bunch of run-down apartments, what people in the city called the labor camps, the projects, *la colonia*. Mostly Mexican field workers and their families lived in these places, and it was inevitable that when the city reached the freeway, which used to be a rural, one-lane road, the apartments would be torn down and something new would replace them. On the opposite side of Hubert's field there was a brand new neighborhood, awash with big, shiny cars and SUVs and green squares of lawn with trees so young they had to be held up by sticks. The sidewalks were white as chalk. In that neighborhood the children from the apartments went to school. They walked along an overpass across the freeway, and they passed the field each morning, and again in the afternoon.

Hubert would watch them walk, and some of the kids walked right across the field, even though the developers had put warning signs that said, "No Trespassing. Violators will be prosecuted."

Usually the kids walked with other kids, but once upon a time there was a little girl named Sara, who walked to school alone. She would walk across the field as if it were her own, private world. She said hello to the gophers, who popped their tiny heads out of their little holes, and sometimes she brought them morsels of food, which she threw near her feet, and they came out to eat.

Every day, twice a day, before and after school, Sara would stop underneath the big oak tree, and she sat there. Sometimes she read, sometimes she sang, but she liked it there in the coolness of the shade. Then one day, out of nowhere — and this is why the tree might have fallen in love with her — Sara stood facing Hubert, staring at the high part of his trunk, as if listening to someone talk.

All was silent expect for the swoosh of the freeway and the laughter of children on their way to school.

Suddenly, Sara stepped back away from the tree, an expression of shock coming across her face. She put her hands over her mouth and started crying. She bawled like a baby, and Hubert felt bad for her, wanted to know what was wrong. After that day, he noticed that she cried a lot. She would come into the field, sit beneath the oak tree and cry. Hubert figured life was hard for the poor girl, and his spirit wanted to comfort her.

Then one day she did something very strange. She stood underneath the great umbrella of Hubert's branches, held her breath, and she held out her arms. She stayed in that stiff position for as long as she could stand it, until her human muscles got sore, and she needed to breathe. It was as if she wanted to be a tree. Everyday she started doing this, standing underneath Hubert, holding up her arms like branches, trying to be a tree. She even began to look like one, and one time, some black birds flying toward her would have landed on her fingers and head, but her muscles got sore and she had to shift her weight and let out a breath, and the birds flew away.

Hubert loved the girl, and he had a big spirit, a great big heart. Have you ever heard of an oak tree with a heart? Well, Hubert's was huge.

He wanted to communicate with the one he loved, but he didn't know human language, so instead he tried other means to get her attention. He dropped leaves like feathers over her shoulders, and he twittered his branches in a breeze, waving his leaves like fingers. He did so many things to get her attention, but Sara didn't seem to understand. She did the same thing everyday. She wept, and then she held her breath and tried to be a tree, until her muscles got too sore and she had to put down her arms.

He dreamed that her parents would buy the house where he would be, and he could be in her backyard and watch her grow and grow and maybe she would become a tree.

Have you ever wanted something so much that you couldn't think of anything else? You can't sleep at night, and the entire world seems to make your desire stronger?

Hubert had it bad for Sara.

He was, as I said, about 150 years old, and he put all of his love, all his tree spirit into wanting to communicate with her, and one day, as she was underneath him, he felt a branch of his move, by his will! Then he found he had about a hundred arms, and he could move them all around, which he did, feeling his own creaky bones.

Sara stood still, trying to be a tree, and she didn't notice that Hubert could move his arms, but he did. Suddenly, on the high part of his trunk, two knot holes became eyes. He could see Sara down there on the ground with her arms out. He could see the same way a human being could see, maybe a bit more blurry, like a movie camera slightly out of focus, looking down on Sara, who sat now, on the ground, her back against the trunk. He saw the top of her head.

"Sara," he said, and right as he willed saying it, a slit for a mouth on his trunk opened up. "Sara?" he said. He could speak!

Sara froze like a tree. In the entire field, the only thing that moved were her eyes in the sockets, looking around for the source of the voice.

"It's me," he said.

"Me?" she said. She turned around, expecting a schoolmate, because the voice of the tree was very young-sounding. Indeed, a tree like Hubert could live for another two hundred years.

"It's me. It's me."

Sara looked up at the tall tree, into the branches, where the sun leaked between the leaves, causing her to squint. He moved a few of his branch-arms, waving his leaves like fingers. "Hello."

"Oh, wow," said Sara, hands over her mouth. "You're alive."

Now, I won't linger on the details of what they said and what brought them to the biggest problem either one of them would ever have. I want to get to the good part, and although you may not believe it, it really happened the way I'm going to tell it. Let me say that they spent each day talking and laughing, telling jokes to one another, reading poetry to each other. Sara curled up around the trunk of Hubert, and he put one of his branch-arms around her, to cradle her neck. They were best friends, or so she thought.

Sara was a girl of 10 years old, so for hours during the day she had to be in school. In the late afternoon, she had to go home. All night Hubert stood in that field waiting for her, weeping for her, yawping so barbarically into the night that the dark orange glow of the encroaching city pulsed to the rhythm of his cries.

Then Hubert learned to walk, slowly at first, like a woman walking in a long skirt too tight at the ankles, but he took the new opportunity and started following Sara to school. "I love you," he said following her down the sidewalk. "I want to be with you always."

Sara turned around and said to him — waving her arms in the air — "Don't you see? You're a tree. I'm a girl."

"But I love you," he said. "Maybe your parents can buy the house that will have me in the backyard."

"Oh, yeah? My parents are poor! We couldn't buy even a house in the worst neighborhood, ever. They can barely pay rent!"

He waited for her on the school grounds and when she was done he followed her home. "Marry me," he said.

Sara had become very mature about relationships, thanks to the *telenovelas* her mother watched. "Look," she said. "You know how I feel about you. But it would never work. What would our children be like?"

"I don't care," he said, "I love you.

"Look, I can't be a tree. No matter how hard I try."

Quite frankly, Hubert went a little too far in what Sara at first thought was a game. He followed her everywhere, showing up at the schoolyard, looking down at her as she ran during P.E with her classmates. It got to the point that she always had to look over her shoulders, wherever she was, hoping that she wasn't being followed. She considered getting an injunction.

The last straw was what happened late one night. She was in the warm roundness of her bedroom, in bed with her three little sisters. She couldn't sleep, and then, suddenly, when she looked out the window, she saw him.

He was looking in at her, smiling, waving his leaves at her, innocent of how his acts bothered her, waving and smiling as if she would be happy to see him. He lightly tapped on the glass. "Sara?" he said. "Hey, Sara!"

Fortunately, her sisters were asleep. Sara got up, went to the window and said, "What are you doing here?"

"Can you come out?"

"*¡Basta ya!*" Sara said.

She found her slippers at the foot of the bed, and, in a white nightgown that went all the way to her feet, she walked out of the front door of the apartments, into the night. Hubert was waiting for her. "Don't you love me, Sara?" he asked.

Sara took one of his hands and led him through the apartment complex. Some teenagers were drinking beer under a streetlight. They crossed the overpass of the freeway and went into the dark, empty field. Signs in the moonlight said "No Trespassing. Violators will be prosecuted."

She led Hubert back to his spot. She stopped.

Hubert was sad. She noticed that his branches were drying out, delicate as chicken bones. His leaves looked wilted and colorless, and he leaned over the field like an old man too exhausted to move. Hubert was going to tell her that they could find a way, they could work it out, please give him a chance at life, but his human language was gone as the slit of his mouth closed up. The eyes on the high part of the trunk were only knots. Not eyes. His branches were stiff. Sara looked at him, at the high part of the trunk — moonlight coming through the branches.

She winced when she saw it again.

She hated it more than anything in the world.

But there it was, just like the first day she had seen it.

Attached to his trunk was a sign posted by the city. It said "Tree removal requested.

"Dangerous, rotting, infected."

The date for removal was the following day.

"If I could be a tree," she said, "I would rather have them take me." She lifted up her arms like a tree, and she held them for a long time, but her muscles got sore and she couldn't hold her breath.

FOUR

EPILOGUE: BORGES AND THE XICAN@ (in b flat)

Je suis ma fils
mon pere, ma mere
et je suis moi.
                                                        A. Artuad

They asked the Chicano questions about Mexico, Cuba, and the pop idol Ricky Martin. They asked him about Day of the Dead, Cinco de Mayo, and *Like Water for Chocolate*. He was expected to be a role model to Latino students, even rich exchange students, whom other faculty mistook for people of his own experience. Once a professor from another department called him and said she had a student from Argentina. Would he be willing to talk with him, maybe give the student some encouragement? Most international students needed little encouragement from someone like him, different class, different culture, but his colleagues assumed it was all the same. He was the campus Latino, El Super Token.

They asked the Chicano questions about Mexico, Cuba, and the pop idol Ricky Martin. They asked him about Day of the Dead, Cinco de Mayo, and *Like Water for Chocolate*. He was expected to be a role model to Latino students, even rich exchange students, whom other faculty mistook for people of his own experience. Once a professor from another department called him and said she had a student from Argentina. Would he be willing to talk with him, maybe give the student some encouragement? Most international students needed little encouragement from someone like him, different class, different culture, but his colleagues assumed it was all the same. He was the campus Latino, El Super Token.

At a department party, the chair casually asked him to teach a class on Latin-American Literature, in translation. "You know, a little magical realism," she said, "Garcia Marquez, Borges."

This short chubby woman in her sixties was bald because of her cancer treatment, and she had a red scarf tied around her head. The flesh of her cheeks jiggled as she talked and sagged as she listened. He liked her a lot — at times he felt a surge of love for her — and he had taken the job so far away from home — in rural Minnesota — because of her. She was a lesbian activist in a small town called Marshall, where they could still be shocked by such open sexuality, and she was one of the least judgmental people he had ever met. She called him Danny, a name he hadn't used since childhood. When she spoke, her cheeks wobbled, and her eyes were focused, grey. "Our students could use a little spice in their literary diet," she said.

"Damn straight," he said. "I'll feed 'em."

"I could use a little more Borges in my life," she said.

He nodded and said, "Who couldn't?" as if he knew what she was talking about. He had never read Borges.

"Maybe next semester you could teach your single-author class on him."

"Man!" he said, shaking his head like he couldn't believe his good luck. "What a class that would be!"

"Hell yeah!" she said, raising her glass for a toast. They were both drunk.

Later on that semester, he went to a bar with the chair and the young creative writing professors. As he drank draft beer, one of them said she had heard he would be teaching a single-author class on Borges, and she asked what works he would be using. He was watching the light sparkle on the curve of his glass, a tiny reflected version of his face, like a funhouse mirror. He shrugged his shoulders and said, "There's so much to choose from."

One young man, a brilliant young poetry professor named Joe, smiled and slapped the table, as if he had a deliciously evil idea. "The man's a fucking genius," he said.

Others agreed. They used words like *erudite* and *brilliant*. The Chicano mumbled some sweeping statement that he wished would swish the old man's image under the rug, and then he changed the subject.

The chair leaned over the table, the ends of her red scarf flapping like rabbit ears, and she said that she would like to sit in on a class or two.

"Me too!" said another colleague.

He said, "Sure. No problem."

The town had no bookstore, so one Saturday morning, he got into his mini-truck with California license plates still on it, and he drove two hours on a two-lane highway through cornfields and past one-street towns, to the nearest city, Sioux Falls, South Dakota, population 90,000. He went to the Barnes and Noble to buy Borges. All they had was an ultra-thin paperback of *Everything and Nothing*, a small collection of stories, less than one hundred pages. He held it in the palm of his hand, walked up to the boy at the counter and asked, as if disappointed, "This is all you have by Borges?"

"Who?" asked the boy.

He didn't think the little, thin book would be enough, not to understand the man, *el gran Borges,* the bard of the River Plate, so he went to the gates of the university library, and walked up the dim winding stairs of stacks of books, and he checked out all he could get by and about Borges, interviews, essays, poetry, and it took him three trips to carry the books up three flights of stairs to his apartment.

He read "Man on Pink Corner," "About the Purple Land," and "The Dead Man." But he couldn't understand, even when he forced himself to read all the way through a long, boring essay on solipsism (a word he had to look up). The old man's words meant nothing to him. He couldn't grasp the dates and references to dead writers. He tried desperately to enter the vivid dream, when a story played like a movie in his head, he tried to walk into "The Garden of Forking Paths," "Nightmares" and "Blindness," "The Lottery in Babylon," "The Meeting in a Dream," "Things that Might have Been." Erudition kept pushing him away. He felt like he was walking through a landscape of words and names and footnotes and italicized phrases in other languages.

The Chicano professor was still young, this his first university position, and he was still developing as a writer, a thinker, a person, still wrestling with his past, still fearful of his future, still able to fall deeply into despair and depression. He decided that his inability to understand Borges was because he was too stupid. It would be worse if he tried to read him in Spanish, because he would have to look up every other word. He couldn't read Spanish.

He remembered his father's words, "Boy, you're a worthless piece of shit."

One Friday night, alone in the rural town, frustrated with Borges, he had nothing to do, so he went to a university football game. He arrived during halftime, while the marching band was taking the field. They wore brown uniforms, and their white band-hats shone under the stadium lights. The PA system announced that they would play a song called "Pachuco." How ironic, he thought, being so far away from Aztlán[1]. He wondered how many of the Minnesotan band members knew that a pachuco was an urban Chicano, a zoot suiter, father of today's cholo. His father had been a pachuco. As a teenager, he had been a wannabe cholo, walking with his friends through the labyrinth of city streets, looking for something to destroy, looking for a way to get drunk or high. As these Minnesotan band members played "Pachuco," did they know that U.S. sailors and the police used to beat up pachucos? Did people here know the difference between a Chicano and other dark-skinned people who they rarely saw in their town? At this game, so many blonde, blue-eyed people sat in the stands that a dark-haired German would have stood out in the crowd. He definitely stood out. People looked at him as he took a seat alone in the stands. He was too different not to attract attention. One woman who looked at him was a staff member from human resources. She waved at him and smiled in that friendly rural Minnesota way.

When he had walked into the human resources office for the first time, she had greeted him with a "Hiya!" Her thick Minnesota accent reminded him of the movie *Fargo.* He told her he was a new employee. "Great!" she said. She asked if he was hired by maintenance.

He said no, that he was a professor of English.

"Isn't that exciting!" she said, like she was happy for him. She helped him fill out his retirement papers.

Now, she and her husband watched the marching band play "Pachuco."

---

1. *The mythical homeland of the Aztecs, believed by Chicanos to be the Southwest United States. California Chicanos often refer to their state as Califaztlán.*

The song was in an up-beat tempo, a swing tune from the Big Band era, and the band members marched in precise lines across the glowing green field. When two lines arched like caterpillars in opposite directions, they became two pulsing circles that slithered down the field like the infinity sign. The bleachers were only a few tiers high, like at a high school, so the maneuver didn't look as spectacular as it might have looked from the sky. But he liked the green of the field, so bright, and so vast in its perfect geometry, and he liked how the marching band helmets shone so white.

Quite frankly, their playing was amateurish, like a high school marching band. The best players left a clarinet behind, which squealed like a child trying to keep up with his parents. The university was on the edge of town, across a field of tall grass, the great Midwestern prairie, treeless for miles, and when the wind came across the plain, it blew hard. It almost blew the tubas from the arms of the players, two of them, one at the end of each marching line, their instruments wobbling in the wind. They held onto those fat, brass bodies like they were giant helium balloons at the Macy's Thanksgiving Day parade, pulling them back down to earth, keeping them from flying away.

He tried to block out the band, the crowd, the field. He pulled out the pocket-sized paperback of *Everything and Nothing* that he had bought in Sioux Falls. He tried to read, but this gathering distracted him, so different from football games in Califaztlán, where Chicanos and Asians and Blacks sat in the bleachers, and where he and his cholo friends stood around smoking cigarettes, away from the lights, next to a chain-link fence.

It felt strange to be a part of the crowd yet apart from the crowd, as if he were glimpsing into another world.

A few tiers in front of him three blonde girls with bobbed hair were watching the band. One of them pointed to a tuba player, who wobbled on the field. She giggled and said, "That's him! That's Jeremy."

The other girls giggled. The one who had pointed at Jeremy wore a jean jacket. On the back was a large red, white and blue patch, a peace symbol, like something from the 1970s, although now in the 2000s the symbol's value was retro fashion. Still, this could look like the late seventies, he thought. If his peripheral vision blurred — as if he were looking through a tunnel — into another time — and if all he saw were these three girls, this could be like when he was in high school. He had gone to the football games. He used to smoke pot under the bleachers. He wore a faded jean jacket, frayed at the sleeves — and it smelled sweet, like old denim — and on the sleeve he had a patch, *Chicano Power!* brown fist and all. It wasn't sewn on, because his mother wouldn't do it for him since she didn't like the patch. She thought it would get him into trouble, that racists would jump him. He stuck it on the arm of the jacket with masking tape, and it often fell off, and he had to push it back on and press hard against his arm until it stuck again. His hair was past his shoulders, straight and black, and his girlfriend was white. Eventually she sewed on the patch for him.

He watched the lady from Human Resources walk over to the girls. She spoke with them and gave one of them money, presumably her daughter. The mother's hair was cut in that same style: a short, blonde, rural-Minnesota bob. When the mother was a teenager, she could have been sitting where her daughter was sitting, pointing to a band member she had known. The mother is the daughter and the daughter is the mother.

The band blared percussion and brass.

"Borges," he told himself.

He didn't care who won the football game and only showed up because as a tenure-track faculty member, he would be seen by university administrators. It would show that he supported the school and was involved with the community. The chair of his department had told him that if he went to a football game, he should save the ticket stub and put it in his tenure review file.

He opened his copy of *Everything and Nothing*.

As the girls giggled, as the band brayed, as the Minnesota wind blew through the bleachers, he read.

> *At first he thought that all people were like him,*
> *but the astonishment of a friend to whom he had*
> *begun to speak of this emptiness showed him*
> *his error and made him feel always that*
> *an individual should not appear different in*
> *outward appearance.*

Suddenly, Borges' words lit up on his face. He felt as if he were meant to read that passage right at that exact moment. The language carried him into the entrance of this story, allowing him inside the Borges dream —no, more —it was *pulling* him inside the dream. Entering the landscape, this other reality, he saw, inside a cottage at night, a man sitting forlornly on his "second-best bed." *Shakespeare* at first "thought all people were like him!" Shakespeare — empty, without identity — hid his despair "in the sub-textual corners" of his famous plays. That was what this story was about, and Borges must have done this with his own writings, hid himself in the shadows of language. The story was about that! He understood that this story about Shakespeare was about Borges, his despair.

A tuba groaned.

The three girls giggled, and the lights went out on the pages and came up again on the football game. He tried to read on, but the wall of language kept him out. He was in darkness again, and there he stood, book with only words in his hands, like in "Araby," a creature driven by vanity. Below him, the three girls giggled at the slow moan of the tuba.

His family was surprised when he told them he was moving to Minnesota. "Have you seen the movie *Fargo*?" they asked him. He told them that he was hired to teach at a university, and it occurred to them that all his years of college might lead to something other than an excuse not to get a job. His father was so happy that he told his son, "Maybe you're not a complete dummy." They had been proud of him being a student, but that life had lasted too long for a working-class family, ten years, during which he was always broke. His mother died when he was still a waiter, before he even got his bachelor's degree, which took him over eight years because he worked long hours and was involved in Chicano activism. She hated the word Chicano.

Earlier in time, when he was in junior high, his family was certain that he would end up in prison or dead. His father always said so. When he was in junior high, he often walked onto his block and saw a police car parked in front of his house. He knew that inside the living room a cop sat with his parents on the couch, waiting for him to get home so they could question him or book him or both. He often sat on the curb hidden by an oak tree, alone, watching his house, watching shadows pass by the windows, his mom, his brother, the police, and he rested his chin on his shoulder, the sweet smell of old denim soothing his spirit.

In seventh grade he sold pot in the boys' bathroom, sweaty eager white kids surrounding him as they held out dollars and said, "Me next." He got arrested by the fire marshal for selling M80s — quarter sticks of dynamite. His father grabbed him by the neck and pushed him against the wall. "I ought to hang you by the balls!" he said.

His father, who had tattoos up and down his arms and on his chest, used to walk around the house in a tank-top undershirt, colloquially called a wifebeater. He acted big and mean to his son, because he was trying to teach him to be someone. The father figured that by telling his son over and over how worthless he was, what a piece of shit he was, how he was good-for-nothing, and, if he occasionally beat him, the son would try harder *not* to be worthless. When the father used the belt, the boy lay scrunched up on the floor, afraid to look up at those angry eyes, at the way his father tightened his lips around his teeth as he whipped the boy. Sometimes when he passed the boy in the hallway of their home, he would raise his hand and hit him and call him an idiot.

After almost flunking out of high school, he had nothing else to do, so he went to community college. Something happened to him there. He suddenly liked studying. He made the dean's list without trying. He transferred to a university and got a B.A. in Political Science, an M.A. in English, and an MFA in Creative Writing. He got a book contract for a collection of stories he called *The Chicano Book of the Dead*. His family was proud. And although they had come to accept the surprise of his "success," to him it felt new and strange, even surreal, and when he went home to visit once or twice a year and he sat with family around the Christmas tree or around the table drinking weak instant coffee, he suddenly rose out of his body. Sound stopped and he observed his family members' gestures as if he were in a time bubble floating by the scene, watching the present from the future or from the past or from some eternal place, like the teenager sitting on the curb looking through the glass of his house, until bang! he heard words again, and he smelled beans and salty pork. He was part of his family again, back at the Formica-topped table crammed into the kitchen.

Recently he had visited Fresno from Minnesota and his father took him to a Chicano pachanga, a big party. "Come and see real Chicanos," he told his son. "You could write about it."

Three generations of urban Chicanos — pachucos, cholos, and gang bangers — gathered in someone's backyard in one of Fresno's poorest barrios. Each generation had tattoos — the one-armed man playing horseshoes; the shirtless viejitos sitting on lawn chairs, drinking beer; the sleepy-eyed teenage boys with tattoo letters on their necks or dog paws tattooed on their foreheads, claiming their allegiance to Los Bulldogs con safos y que. And all generations smoked yesca, marijuana, except for his father and him. But they both drank a lot of beer from the keg, and with a Styrofoam cup in one hand and his other arm around his son's shoulder, the father led his boy around the backyard and introduced him to his compadres and the children and grandchildren of his compadres. He said, "This is my son. He has a book. He's a professor in Minnesota."

He wanted his father to stop mentioning the book and the job, because he was certain he was the only writer there, the only professor among upholstery workers and janitors and the unemployed, and he didn't want to appear different. "Don't, Dad," he pleaded. "Stop saying I have a book."

The father looked his son in the eyes, as if facing his own reflection in the mirror. "But I'm proud of you," he said.

He wrote and published stories, but he often felt like a phony, like he didn't belong at the university or in the pages of lit mags and would be better off or at least more at peace if he were a worker like his father and he should have kids and should be married and should drink beer from Styrofoam cups, and, mostly, he should be living in Fresno and having parties in backyards which overlooked alleys with stray dogs. He doubted the veracity of his intellect and thought that maybe he had fallen through Affirmative Action cracks.

After the football game, he walked forlornly up the three flights of stairs to his attic apartment. Borges books were stacked around the living room, against the walls, on the tables, on the TV. He began to reread *Everything and Nothing*, hoping that the feeling of understanding that had touched him at the football game would return, but nothing. Everything was nothing. He read Norbert's analysis on Borgian language,[2] in which he argues that Borges, seeing circular time, captures the eternal artistic soul, the Source, he calls it, which the artist receives through color, image, and sound. Every detail — since it contains God — has the same qualities as Borges's Aleph, a point in space that simultaneously contains all images, outside of time, all times spinning around like electrons in empty space. Norbert uses an example of an Aleph-like detail that he found in multiple works of literature and visual art: a

2. *Norbert, François,* Tous les reves en tous les temps. *(1979).*

single tree on a hill. That eternal tree is being seen from so many perspectives by so many artists that to see all of them at once would be like seeing the tree spinning around and around, like a star, like sparkling geometry, crystalline, precise, an Aleph. Around the spinning image, generations of writers and artists gather, but they stand outside of time. Most may not be cognizant of the power and energy they are admitting into their work, but they feel it, the connection. They are members of a community created from beauty.

The Chicano let the book slide down his chest. He didn't get it. He didn't want to get it. It was boring. His eyes got heavy. He dozed off for a few seconds. He saw — in flashes of dream imagery — an endless hallway of books, like dark streets of skyscrapers in a surrealist painting. He saw himself walking the labyrinthine streets of a red city of books.

Suddenly, his eyes popped open like being pitch-forked by the devil.

He saw the books piled in the middle of the floor, as if some religious cult was ready to burn them. He stood up, threw the books on his desk into the pile, and looked around for matches, as if he would light them, but he was barely coming out of a dream. He felt anger, and he needed to do something to that pile of books on his floor, something. He heard a bang on his window, a branch from a giant tree hitting glass. The wind outside shook the branches, like in the last dance of Sara's oak tree. He opened all the windows in the four directions of the apartment. The wind was mad. The wind blew papers off his desk, blew his hair in a mess, it slapped the Chicano Movement posters on his walls against the walls — sand coming in from the screens — dirt coming in — the spirit of earth swirling in the air like imps — like the demons Herod invokes with violas in

L'enfance du Christ. He stood before the pile of blowing books — pages flapping — his Indian nostrils taking in the burnt smell of corn from the processing plant.

"I hate you," he yelled to the pile, picturing Borges on the floor in a fetal position, and he kicked the old man in the ribs, books flying around like dying pigeons.

Borges was a bourgeois bastard who didn't care about the people. The Chicano was involved with the Movement, and he knew that Borges remained silent throughout the Dirty Little War, when thousands of young people disappeared "for questioning" by the government and never returned. It seemed Borges cared little about the oppressed, let alone the revolution. Borges wasn't in love with justice, he was in love with metaphor. Can metaphor save the oppressed? Is metaphor, like bread, for the people?

Fact: Borges's father was a writer. And although the elder Borges got little recognition and published only one book, *El Caudillo* — which he distributed for free among friends — to be around words and books as a child could not but make Georgie at home among words and books and ideas in books. The Borges family traveled to France and Switzerland, where they settled for a time, and Georgie learned German and French, in addition to his two native languages, English and Spanish[3]. Georgie spent hours in his father's library, randomly pulling books from the shelves. He read on an overstuffed armchair in the study, as the other children played outside his window, yelling out their games, their laughter, which he was accustomed to ignore.

His childhood was a made up of street lamps and dogs. His father watched the evening news, before falling asleep shirtless on the couch. The Chicano child didn't

---

3. *His grandmother was English, and as a child he spoke English and was called Georgie, not Jorgecito.*

read, unless he was forced to by those kindly, sinister beings[4], public school teachers. He read books like *Danny and the Dinosaur* and *The Star-Bellied Sneeches*. When he was a teenager, he still hated to read, preferring to get stoned and drink bottles of wine on the banks of the city's dry canals. He liked running across freeway overpasses and throwing rocks at the cars that passed below, he liked to watch TV reruns of *Bewitched, Lost in Space, The Land that Time Forgot*.

Now, in his apartment in rural Minnesota, he walked in a circle, around and around the pile of books, and then he walked through all the rooms, the bedroom, the dining room, the living room, he walked past the bad breath of open windows, feeling his momentum rise, wanting to feel some swirl of energy that might make him so alert that he would understand Borges. But nothing happened. He slumped in his arm chair and tried to read Borges, but he couldn't focus on the old man's words.

As the wind blew his hair, he read "The Library of Babel."

When it was announced that the library contained all books (Sometimes as he read, the universe faded away, the arm chair where he sat, and the shelves of books lining his walls disappeared) *the first reaction was unbounded joy* (as he entered the world of the book, into the vivid and continuous dream, like a movie.) *All men felt themselves possessors of*

---

4. *See Octavio Paz'* Labyrinth of Solitude, *where he claims that North American children are constantly exposed to brief formulas, the books they read at school, TV shows and commercials, etc, which only consider the positive aspects of reality, that avoid pain and suffering. Therefore, he may be at a disadvantage to begin with, in that his thoughts have been shaped to be linear and formulaic. "A person imprisoned by these schemes is like a plant in a flowerpot too small for it: he cannot grow or mature."*

an intact and secret treasure. There (No, reading was more than a movie playing in his head, because fiction that goes from scene to scene is) *was no personal problem whose elegant solution did not exist –somewhere in some hexagon* (how shall we say it, is voyeuristic, Cortázar's quote, or like Malamud wrote, metaphorically thin? He liked that) *the universe was justified: the universe suddenly became congruent with the unlimited width and breadth of humankind's hope. At that period* (the slow part of reading, to stop on images, like they were paintings in a museum). *There was much talk of the Vindication* (he liked lingering with the artist; he could evoke the yellow flower while reading literature enough to smell it, he could imagine caressing a fat, eternal cat.) — *books of* apolgea *and prophesies that would vindicate* (He could walk with a murderer and a fool into an underground labyrinth of cold stone. Now, the Chicano professor loved to read, and if he was impatient with what he read, he would be impatient with what he wrote.

Reading should be like entering different rooms of a house, creating walls that rise up around you and then dissolve into a mountain range or a tree on a hill.) *for the time the actions of* (Yet all he could do with Borges was peek inside a blurry window or a dark doorway into the room, never able to enter) *every person in the universe and that held wondrous* (because he feared too much as he read, unable to focus, feared being stupid, not good enough, unworthy to receive the gift of art.)

> *Thousands of greedy individuals abandoned their sweet native hexagons and rushed downstairs, upstairs, spurred by the vain desire to find their vindication. These pilgrims squabbled in the narrow corners , muttered dark imprecations*

What he saw that night when he was trying to understand Borges was a plastic landscape. Words and symbols unfolded around him, as if language were a tarp keeping him in the back of a pickup truck. He remembered the video images of the Riverside County Sheriff deputies beating the farmworking Mexican lady with their clubs, over and over again. There must be a literary counterpart to that image, some archetypal meaning for him in relation to that image. The cop's billy club is language.

Near Tijuana, on the California side of the freeway, were yellow signs warning of illegal aliens running across the busy lanes, the image of a mother running, holding her child's hand, her child holding a doll, all three figures running. And when he saw that image he always thought it would make a good T-shirt. The caption would read "Late for class." That's why the lady's running, because she's late to class.

In high school, he hated classes.

Hated anything with structure.

Anything white, except for his girlfriend Amy Morris.

He was reading, but he imagined himself opening a door and entering a dark parking lot with rows of new cars. He felt like he was on a stage, a silver-blue night scene, and he stood alone among the cars. But suddenly, white lights snapped on, and appearing from the darkness, his teenage friends walked over to him. They walked like hoodlums (*I have seen two of them, which refer to persons in the future, persons perhaps*) toward the bright bowling alley entrance, their shadows stretched by the lights, splayed over the hoods of new cars, his arm around Amy Morris. With his free hand, he snapped off the antennas of every car he passed, snap, snap, snap. His friends laughed, and Amy laughed.

The Chicano put down the book. He hadn't understood a word.

He fell asleep. What happened next was the dream. This was the dream that finally did it. It was in *that* world that he finally got a glimpse of Borges.

He dreamed a mob of books was closing in on him, like evil trees in a magic forest. Some laughed, some sneered or mocked him. He found himself pressed against a chain link fence threatened by giant copies of *Parallel Lives, Confessions, The Idiot*.

He screamed and the scene changed and he saw an old man standing before a mirror, reading a thin book, laughing. He approached closer, but in the reflection of the mirror, he saw his own Indian face staring back at him.

But here's the thing: It wasn't *him* in the mirror, not the present him, not the Chicano professor in rural Minnesota, but him as a teenager, long hair and denim jacket with Chicano Power patch[5].

The old man was engrossed in the book he was reading. That was when the dreamer saw the book's title, *The Chicano Book of the Dead*.

It was a thin book. So light. All that work and it was so small. The first time he had seen it, he held it in his hands like a sick bird. "This is it?" he had said to himself. "This booklet is my book?"

Now, reading the Chicano's book, Borges chuckled.

The Chicano knew he wasn't good, the Chicano knew what the Chicana poet Lorna Dee Cervantes called "that nagging preoccupation that I'm not good enough."

---

5. *And he remembers watching Amy's hands as she sewed on the Chicano Power patch, her face scrunched up in concentration.*

His work had no place in any library. He was a joke. To think he could write something worthwhile — how naïve! And to think of Borges reading his book. He would think the reading of it a waste of time.

But the Chicano had to write. He, frankly, had no choice, because if he didn't write what else would he do? He'd have to get a life, maybe start a family, and perhaps that scared him more than anything else.

He looked at Borges looking into the mirror. "What do I do? I want to understand you. I want to write."

"I'm like you," said the old man. "I want to understand me."

"What do I do?"

"Nothing." Borges closed the book. He put on his glasses and strained to see the Chicano writer, but he was blind and could only see blurs, a formless face.

"Thanks, Chicano," Borges said. "You've been a great influence on my work."

"But I came after you."

"Don't be so linear. If it weren't for you I would have never written 'Everything and Nothing.'"

"I'm. . .I'm the Shakespeare character? It's based on *me?*"

"Don't flatter yourself. I mean that this story you're writing now, or this essay — or this whatever-you-call-it — these words you weave are giving me an idea. Follow me."

"Where are we?" the Chicano asked, looking around as they entered the orange city at night, where skyscrapers were made of books.

"How would I know?" said Borges. "Am I the dreamer or the dreamed?"

A starry sky appeared above their heads. They stood at the edge of a lit up football field, so green, and the band marched like tin soldiers on the horizon, but all was silent, and the stands were dark and empty. "I loved that thing about the football game," Borges said. "That's why you got chills, because I understood what *you* saw."

"But. . .What did I see?"

"Savant l'enfant qui sait qui est son père."

"But. . ."

Borges opened his mouth and out came a ring.

The phone. Sitting on a coffee table. He stood up and walked across the hardwood floor and picked it up. "Hello?"

"Hi, Danny. I called to ask how your classes are going." It was the department chair. "Are you finding yourself adjusting to life in Minnesota?"

"Yeah. How are you?"

"Well, you know.. . the treatment leaves me feeling like shit. But other than that."

"Hey, look," said the Chicano. "You want to go get a beer?"

"Uh, yeah, that sounds good," she said. He pictured the red scarf around her head, billowing in the Minnesota wind.

The next time he went into Borges, he didn't look for meaning or expect the form of the stories to fall together in a way that he could explain to students; rather he entered the unending rooms of his imagination, his own imagination, looking for Borges. He knew that beyond all the words and italics and the apocryphal scholarship was a lonely old man who liked to talk, who liked to walk, *a solitary man for whom solitude was unbearable,* a man who hid himself, his soul, in the sub-textual corners of the work. All you had to do was enter into the place where language is made, and his spirit would be released into your spirit.

The Chicano glimpsed him reading under a 100-year-old oak tree. And many times, when he caught up with Borges, he also found himself, the boy with the jean jacket, Chicano Power patch shining like hope on his sleeve. They hung out in walled gardens, walking, talking, sometimes reading aloud to each other, Borges and the Chicano.

ACKNOWLEDGMENTS

Some of these stories have appeared in the following journals, *Rock and Sling*, *The Dos Passos Review*, *Palabra*, *Fresno's Undercurrent*, *Pachuco Children Hurl Stones*, *Flyway*, *Colere*, *Bordersenses*, and the forthcoming anthology *Literary El Paso*. I would like to thank the editors of all these journals as well as all those who helped me put together this book, especially Sasha Pimentel Chacón, Kenneth Chacón, John Hales, Jack Boyd, Dave Hurst, Matt Espinoza, Joann Villalobos, Stacy Brand, Tim Z. Hernandez, Trent Hudley, the incredibly brilliant students of the Puente Program, and my friends and students from California State University, Fresno and University of Texas, El Paso. I'd also like to thank the folks at Black Lawrence Press, especially Diane Goettel, Colleen Ryor, and Sarah Crevelling.